The Wild Adventures of Faithy

By Peggy Mercer

Best Wishes,
Peggy Mercer

Peggy Mercer

Visit the following links:

http:// m l w i l s o n p u b l i s h i n g . w e e b l y . c o m

www.facebook.com/michaellwilsonjrbooks

Swamp Town Publishing LLC

ARCHER, FLORIDA

First Edition

ML Wilson Publishing LLC

Archer, FL 32618

https://mlwilsonpublishing.weebly.com/

Drawings : Michael Wilson Sr.

Publisher's Note: This is a work of fiction. Names, characters, places, and incidents are a product of the author's imagination. Locales and public names are sometimes used for atmospheric purposes. Any resemblance to actual people, living or dead, or to businesses, companies, events, institutions, or locales is completely coincidental.

The Wild Adventures of Faithy / **Peggy Mercer** -- 1st Ed.

Dedication

For my Cousins, who were there,

especially Uveda, Ceelee, Joan, Janice,

Donna Ann and in memory of Pat, who

were sisters more than cousins and for

the boys, Donald, Gary, Mark, Timmy

and Jimmy, Larry, Donnie and the

others.

Table of Contents

Acknowledgement

I wish to thank Mike Wilson at Swamp Town Publishing, Archer, Florida, for his hard work. As usual it is close to perfect. I also wish to thank his father, Michael Wilson Sr, for the drawings they are wonderful.

Chapter 1

Going, Going, Gone Country

It is my first time ever going to Searock City to visit grandma, grandpa and all my country cousins without Mama and Papa. I am nine point five years old and I am going on this vacation alone. Papa was all for it. Mama was all against it and I was very much siding with mama. There are many reasons. Stay with me.

Papa says, "Do her good down on the farm. She'll get better out there in the fresh air." Good at what? I wondered. Better at what? I was already good at lots.

Mama says, "Faithy Jane is very frail. Why, she may get hurt!"

"I don't wanna go. I'm ah, not like my cousins," I say and shot Mama a *help* look.

"But your cousins love you, honey and they can't wait to see you! It's the Easter holiday and you're never too big to hunt eggs. You'll have real clean fun and who knows what all y 'all might get into!" says Papa.

"Yes, and she may get more than eggs," Mama sighs. "I do not like this." She crosses her arms and I cross mine. Papa dances around the kitchen smiling. He is winning.

"She's nine and a half. Time for her to enjoy life with other children. Which means river woods and grandma's house. I grew up down yonder on the river and I loved it and I know Faithy Jane will love it too!"

"My stars, Linton. If all they did out there was snap beans and milk cows, I'd be all for it, but you know how er, wild all those country children are!" Mama banged the grits pot with a wooden spoon as she complained.

"Now don't talk bad about my folks, Lettie. I don't want our only daughter spoiled rotten. She needs to get dirt under her nails; toughen up!" Papa shouted. "Today's world calls for tough kids!"

I cringe, dirty fingernails? Yuck! I don't want to be tough. I like being a bit, ah, pampered as Mama calls it. I am an only child which should count for something!

My fingernails get a mini manicure once a month when mama takes me to the local spa. As far as being tough, aren't straight A's enough? Because in 4th (this past year), I nailed those magnificent A's. Also, I was top Accelerated Reader. Add to this--drum roll here--I won the county spelling bee. Also, I was Miss Citizenship every time the gold-plated pins went around. How much tougher (smarter) does Papa want?

I have a dog, Swede, and a cat, Tweed, and a best friend, Uveda, whom I talk to on the phone 24/7. None of this takes a steel spine, I know, I know, but at the time of this weird conversation, I really wanted to stay at 203 Old Rusty Street safe in our house in Busted Knuckle, Georgia. (Busted Knuckle is in fact, the town's real name.)

Right now, at Busted Knuckle, dogwoods are popping like popcorn and azaleas look on fire with blooms. Hedges are clipped and everybody acts semi-normal.

On the other hand, every time I have visited grandma's house at Searock City, something life threatening usually occurs and about always to you-know-who! If it can go wrong, it does.

And I am always "it" and have to, as country folks say, eat crow.

My country cousins' favorite pastime seems to be picking on me, who they call their city slicker cuzz or Miss Goody Two Shoes.

"Well, maybe she'll find herself and grow up some," Mama says softly, and I know that I am going, going, gone country! Whatever awaits me, call it fate, destiny or the luck of the draw, I am going for it.

Sure enough, Easter week arrived, and I was fairly tossed out at Searock City near the Satilla River. My world shrunk to the size of a black-eyed pea rolling down a four-lane highway.

I will never forget standing on grandma's front porch that night, watching papa and mama drive back the way they came. Papa's toy, a restored 1967 gold Cutlass convertible kicked up dust and he shouted, "Who wants to be a country girl, ha ha ha!"

Now I thought, it is only Monday and Easter Sunday is a week away, which may as well be four-score and seven! I am stranded at Grandma and Grandpa Searock's. I have six days to find myself; as mama put it, grow up and get healthy, as papa put it but to me this means life or death, sink or swim! To me, I have been delivered here to be eaten alive by my country cousins, those pestering meanies who think they know it all.

Oh, I am an unhappy camper and this Easter Week vacation at Grandma's has not even started. Hello misery. Hello, stuck in the sticks! The country, whoopee!

And now, laugh if you must, but reader, keep your smeller to this book because this is not your normal upper reader. It is highly ab-normal like Dracula normal or something.

It is the almost unbelievable true story which I will here-to-for call: The Wild Adventures of Faithy (that's me!). Little do y 'all know!

Chapter 2

Never Let Them See You Sweat

Facing the fact, I am with my blood kin at Searock City is enough to make me blanch. It is important y 'all visualize the cold hard truth. Even at age nine point five, and I understand folks are who they are because of where they live; how they're raised. It's all about something called genealogy or roots. So, I will try and paint a picture of this place where my life and times had a head-on collision with the next Century.

Here, at Searock City there are seven farmhouses. Six of the houses are square and made of old gray weathered wood; clapboard they call it. The six houses are lined up like Monopoly houses on Park Avenue, except here it is called the Satilla River Road. These houses have a life of their own due to the fact they are occupied by my blood kin, and my blood kin are country folks. Plain as the freckles on my face.

Grandma Lolly and Grandpa Liston and my unique Great

Granny, whom we call her Blue Haired Lilac (in other words, her hair matches her name) lives in the main house (number seven or the Big House) at the bottom of the rise. The big house squats on cinder blocks like a hen setting eggs. On either side of the wide, long front porch are black cherry trees, full of berries and more birds than an aviary—aviary's a great word—told y 'all I get A's!

Cut to my very first morning at grandma's house by the Satilla River. I am still in a fog from last night's trip and late arrival. Sleepy yet wide awake! Fear does this!

"Faitheeeeee Jaaaannnnnee! Are you in there?" It is the voice of my cousin, Budgie, age 11, who has flames for hair and bangs. Her red curls pop up beyond a slightly raised bedroom window. "Faithy, we ain't got all day!" she yells, tapping. At the window is my worst nightmare. I scuttle back against the pillows and clutch the covers. A sea of smirking, double-dog-dare-ya faces crowd Budgie at the window. I mean

there is a whole army of country cousins. Tap, tap, tap! I am outnumbered.

Budgie grins sternly like a teacher. She calls herself a Future Teacher of America and loves us playing school. She holds classes in the pack-house and marks her students (us) pretend desks with tobacco sticks from another century.

I dig out from under a handmade blue quilt and bolt for the door. I push the big skeleton key into the brass lock and hop back into Grandma Lolly's four poster bed.

I yell or croak, "I need my sleep! Doctor's orders!" My knees knock. Outside, Grandpa Liston's rooster, Yellow Boy, crows *Help! Help!*

"Come on, the boys have something to show you!" Budgie shouts.

"Me and Roper want to show you something!" yells Doobie, Budgie's little brother.

He pushes himself up with one hand on Budgie's head. "Come see what we got!"

I didn't want to see! Doobie dreams day and night of stuff to get into. He collects rocks and loves throwing them. Nobody hangs around when Doobie has a rock in his hand.

Roper is Doobie and Budgie's older brother (but in the same grade as Doobie and me, 4th last year but going into 5th next fall). At the window he jumps up and down.

"I been waitin' by this door all morning," wails Lilly, who is five and a half years old and going to first grade next year. She is outside the bedroom door. She calls louder, "You gonna live your whole life in there?" Little Lilly has real blonde hair (like mine), blue eyes, dimples; the works. She is the only cousin who is nice to me.

The doorknob rattles. Outside, Yellow Boy crows *Help! Help!* At the window the faces disappear. Ut-oh, this means something, and I shiver. Goose bumps.

Now, beyond the bedroom door, Doobie yells, "Move. I'll give it my Chuck Norris roundhouse kick!" Feet shuffle. There is fussing, "He pushed me. She pinched me. Move over y 'all!"

Budgie laughs and orders, "Noooooo. Y 'all stop. Faithy's just playing possum. Grandma Lolly's gonna get her outta yonder."

No sooner said, then Grandma Lolly opens the door and steps inside. She winks at me. "Faithy, honey child, stop hiding and come on. If they mess with you, I'll tan their hides. Why, it's Easter Week when the Lord rose from the grave. Your Grandpa Liston's bringing the Easter Sermon on Sunday. So, you must understand, it's a special week!"

Grandma Lolly keeps a hand on the doorknob. She is dressed in jeans, a white t-shirt with red block letters *Jesus Patrol* and a fishing cap with hooks. She smells like maple flavoring and fried bacon. Little Lilly comes into the room, carrying a rag doll.

I sit up in the middle of the bed and lean back on my elbows. I stare at the doorknob and go, "I thought the, er, door was locked. I mean...I did put in the key."

Grandma Lolly laughs, "Ha. Ha. Ha. Honey, them old doors ain't never worked. Ain't a door in this whole house will lock!"

Little Lilly looks up at grandma Lolly, "Tell Faithy 'bout the hobo who come into the house at midnight."

Grandma Lolly laughs, "I'll be telling it later, child. Come on, Faithy!" Then Budgie pushes into the room as Grandma Lolly adds, "Faithy, don't be no fraidy cat. You'll love the river woods without your mama and papa. You'll get to do all kinds of neat stuff."

That's what I am afraid of. No joke.

Budgie stands at the foot of the bed. She brushes her bangs with a broken brush. She says, "You can borrow my brush if you'll give it right back." She does not offer the brush. She just stares at me, smiling.

I look a sight, I think. My chin is too square, my nose is too tipped, and my face is too freckled. I try and smooth down my paper-white blonde hair. Back home, my best friend, Uveda, puts mayonnaise on my hair to make it lay flat. She said if mayo can't calm it down nothing can.

Doobie squeezes into the room and bumps Budgie. He is my age, nine, but taller than any nine-year-old I've ever seen. He wears faded jeans, a green shirt--with the words: ***John Deere Tractor***--and no shoes. His pockets bulge with rocks; ut-oh.

Outside the window, Yellow Boy ar-ah-ar-arrrhhhrrrs *Help!
Help!*

Doobie leans forward and whispers, "You gotta hurry
Faithy, hurry! Me and Roper's got something to show you.
Come on!" He grabs my foot and I kick his hand loose. Ha. Ha.
Chuck Norris Faithy!

This leads Grandma Lolly to shoo Budgie, Doobie and Little
Lilly from the room so I can get out of bed and dress. Little do
they know how I saw war when I got here, or before, so I, the
soldier, have slept with my clothes (battle gear) on. I am ready, I
think.

I slept in my jeans and American Idol t-shirt and oh yeah,
my pearls. I've been nowhere in near memory without my
pearls. I mean, I wear them to school every day.

I jump off the bed. I feel a bit woozy but make a face and
smile tiredly.

I pull on a purple sweater and shiver although it is not cold.
Remember, it is springtime, April, here in the unfriendly South.

I pull open the door and near 'bout get whiplash looking

down the long dimly lit hallway. On the walls are family pictures and little wooden signs: *Welcome, Granny's Kitchen, Laundry, Push Here, If No One Answers, Do it Yourself. Kiss the Cook.   One sign says, If you are out of choices, be brave!*

My cousins clog the end of the hallway. They cheer and yell "Come on! Come on!" I place my right foot then left foot, right, left, right, left, walking the plank.

From the end of the hallway Doobie grunts something he can no longer **not** grunt, "Faithy! Faithy! Me and Roper's caught a coachwhip!"

I stumble into Grandma Lolly's flour-cloudy, maple-bacon smelling kitchen. Grandma Lolly is cooking hotcakes on a flat iron griddle and homemade maple syrup steams in a pot on the stove.

I finger my pearls and ask, "What's a coachwhip?" Not good.

This sets off Great Granny Blue Haired Lilac, who, until this moment, seems asleep in a wheelchair in the corner. Now, she sits straight up and cusses like a sailor. Except she has a way of bleeping her choicest words because Grandpa Liston is a Pentecostal preacher who won't allow belly-achin' or cussing, even from a near 'bout 100year old.

Now, Great Granny Blue Haired Lilac yells at the top of her lungs, "I told them young'uns not to mess with them bleep... bleep... coach whips! Tell Liston to break me a bleeping... gall berry switch! I'm a-gonna whoop their bleeps... till they turn purple!"

Great Granny Blue Haired Lilac is still the most powerful person on knob hill. She and Great Grandpa Lawson (long dead) built this house many moons ago. Yep, this family of mine is steeped sharper than tacks in longevity and stories galore. So, see, Great Granny Blue Haired Lilac is fine in her many hairclips and can of snuff in her apron pocket.

It is easy to see why this house and surroundings are known far and wide as Searock City. I mean, the Searock family is very well known in these parts.

The big house is surrounded by dagger-sharp palmetto bushes. The briar bushes beside the split rail fence are so sharp they will claw your legs till you bleed within an inch of your life. And the pine trees, Jeez. They are taller than the Rural Electric Company (R.E.A) light poles. Now, this is tall!

The morning rolls in like a clip from an old two-tone movie. It is easy to see how my country cousins are feared by city kids who do not understand this way of life. I know I do not and they are my own kin-folks! .

And Reader, this family's confusion did not start today; no. The confusion has been here for a long time for several reasons, main one being the family name.

This family main name was once Seawright. But when Grandma Lolly married Grandpa Liston she became fascinated by his red barn on which someone had painted *See Rock City.* Next thing, Grandma Lolly had paid a town lawyer to change the family name from Seawright to Searock! Hello? I didn't even know you could do such things. I mean, *change* the name you are born with? Get out!

Personally, names are something you are given at day one, birth, such as freckles, or attached ear lobes. Personally, it's just flat out weird to change a name. Unless when you get married or become a movie star and want to go undercover so as to avoid autographs. Or become a spy or join the mafia and need 'bout a half dozen aliases.

And if this is not weird enough Reader, you must see the sign at the end of the river road. It is painted **Searock City** with an arrow beneath it: **O P E N for BUSINESS and Population xxx** (the numbers being scratched through.)

Now and then one of the Searock clan leaves for bigger bushes and brighter berries which is to say parts unknown, at which time someone minuses the population number.

When they return, sooner than later, someone adds a number back. This means the sign **Searock City** stays pretty mucked up. Plus, the bird shot holes. So, the sign looks like it's been beat with a claw hammer and scrawled on with graffiti.

In each yard of the six houses on the River Road are other signs: *Notary Republic* (one Uncle's take on it) and then, *Grease Monkey Garage, at house number two. We Pick up Pecans on Halves* (which means keep half of them for pay) at house number three and so on.

Stuff is in the yards too. Plastic pink flamingos, cement deer, squirrels, ducks and cement blocks line the dirt driveway. Flat tires circle Old Maid flowers and Petunias.

John Deere tractors sit in the fields beyond the houses. In the side yards are cars with their hoods raised. The windows in the cars are busted and the cars are propped up on blocks. Sometimes smaller children will play in these cars for hours. Lights hang from ropes tossed around tree limbs. Men stand around staring under these car hoods, scratching their heads and armpits. They laugh a lot and the cars get old and rusty, and never get fixed.

Out here in the boonies, hound dogs make racket day and night and young'uns hide in azalea bushes big as sapling trees. Goats eat grass out of the yards so there's no need for lawn mowers. In fact, there are no lawns. There are yards, folks, but no lawns.

I've always felt left out in the cold when I visit here. And I have never liked my cousins' jokes. I mean, the jokes seem always on me. Even when Mama and Papa are around, I am always scratching hives and sweating raindrops. I always wonder, am I going to live through this?

Personally, I can see this Easter week is shaping up to be a doozy.

I am terrified. Will my parents ever come back for me? Or will they arrive too late to save me. At any rate, if I go down the tube this Easter week vacation, I'll go down fighting. I mean, I am top reader in my school, and I won the Miss Citizenship pins. I am not a wimp and I need to win whatever fate has for me this time...this time...because one thing I have learned this in school, never let them see you sweat.

Chapter 3

Fraidy Cat Faithy Takes a Stand

This day of doom comes into focus. I stare at the plate of hotcakes. I stare at the fork in my right hand. I smile and choke down a bite. It is hard to swallow while gagging and all eyes are on me. The eyes wait for me to make a move. I am on the hot seat and the day has not even begun. But reader, it is trying to.

Grandma Lolly says, "Young'uns, y 'all let Faithy eat first."

Great Granny Blue Haired Lilac mutters she needs her a gall berry switch. Budgie leans close to my ear and whispers, "You gone eat till the world ends?"

Little Lilly's blonde head nudges me and she says, "A coachwhip's the biggest black snake you ever saw. He's a monster. But I won't let him get you if you'll let me wear your beads. Purdy please with a cherry on top?"

I sigh. "Ok, but they're not beads. They are real pearls. Don't you know pearls?" I wince at my own words. She's just a little kid; she can't help it.

"Okie dokie then, pearls. Gimme please," she begs, holding out her small hands.

"Come on Faithy. We wanta show you something," Doobie says over one shoulder as he leaves the kitchen. Budgie, and another cousin who'd come in, Skeeterhawk, run through the kitchen door on the heels of Doobie and Roper.

Grandma Lolly shoos me out. "Go on darling." She yells after the others, "Y 'all don't aggravate Faithy now. She ain't brave like y 'all are."

Ain't brave? Snakes? No kidding.

Personally, I'd rather have my eyes glued shut than look at a snake. I'd rather be force-fed liver or dye my hair purple and be hauled to the principal's office like the meanest boy in Busted Knuckle Elementary School who did just that.

But then again, this whole story here at Searock City isn't only about some dumb snake. It is about something bigger. No kidding. It is about me living or dying, about my life and times this week. A week to end all weeks. My gut feelings are right; never wrong. Ask mama.

I am rather sick, or so they (the doctors) say, with something called a heart murmur. I am the only cousin who has this, so yeah, I'm special. That is to say everybody has always walked on eggshells around me. *Puny, frail, watch out for her, take care of her, don't let her overdo it, make sure she eats right*, all my life I've heard these warnings day and night, night and day.

The doctors say, this won't hurt you, and it hurts. They say, you can do this and then Mama says, "No, she can't. Why, she may get hurt!"

The doctors say, she'll feel better next month, and I don't. Well, not much. And even if I do feel better, well, Mama foils me by reporting I am not in fact, better. Jeez. How can I win like this? I shy away from that negative junk.

So, I really do NOT, and that's a big **N O T,** trust the guys in white. All this confusion has me wondering if I will ever get well or not.

Now this week! Yep, I think, as I stand up from Grandma Lolly's kitchen table, this morning isn't only about a coachwhip snake. It is about being afraid of being afraid.

It is about how my country cousins have always treated me, Faithy, like I am a wimp who is afraid of her own shadow. At Busted Knuckle elementary they (classmates) whisper the same thing behind my back. I can just sense it.

They talk about me because I am forced to sit and watch the others play. Because I have to rest while they run, jump, scream and have fun at recess. No kidding and because I get what they call special treatment they nick-name me stuff like wimp. Which personally makes me sad and you know, I am determined to somehow overcome this wimpiness.

Yep, I have a truckload of fear in me. But since I am here, I need to prove a thing or two. I know in my heart that I need to stand up for once in my life and be counted. Reader, I need a kick of courage like being kicked by a South Georgia mule.

I follow little Lilly out the door and down the hall. The boys blaze the trail. They are singing to the choir, I think. I am on to them. I am on to their game of traumatize Faithy!

So, with Great Granny Blue Haired Lilac bleeping behind me, I follow Budgie out the front door. Little Lilly pulls my hand.

The boys run down the steps and across the yard. They look back over their shoulders to make sure we are coming.

"Are you a Fraidy Cat, Faithy?" Little Lilly asks as she skips.

"Nah, she ain't no Fraidy Cat, Little Lilly," answers Budgie. "Faithy's just shy."

Grandma Lolly, who is behind us, says, "Faithy will be okay if y 'all young'uns will stop your tom foolery. Somebody break me a good long switch to have handy!"

"Don't be scared, Faithy," vows Little Lilly. "I'll take care of you."

"But hello trouble if you don't like snakes," adds Budgie, brushing her bangs. She's got a smile like she knows something the rest of us don't know and don't need to know!

"Well, I mean who does like snakes? Not me for sure. I am some dumb but not plumb dumb!" I shrug like whatever.

"They just wanna show off," says Little Lilly.

"No kidding," I smell bird feathers and wonder where the rooster is hiding.

But I walk toward the barn, toward my first "test" of living the country life. My first "test" of bravery, argh, the coachwhip snake exam. And despite the fact I sweat raindrops under my armpits and my knees knock plus chewing my tongue I am hoping I can shuck the Fraidy-Cat label. Yep, I want to shuck it for once and all.

I want to find myself, as mama says. I've got to somehow live through this and do some growing up. It is now or never. It is my chance. I am on the hot seat.

And although I have no clue as to how horrible a coachwhip snake really is, and I have zero desire to find out, bum-bum-bum, here comes Fraidy-Cat Faithy to take her stand.

I need to show my country cousins once and for all that I, Faithy, am not a rock to be rolled over, tossed aside, and or shattered with a hammer of fear. I could meet Dracula right now and I would try not to flinch!

Chapter 4

Faithy vs the Coachwhip

We walk toward the barn. Budgie and Little Lilly pull me along. Little Lilly chatters, "Doobie's the bestest snake charmer. The snakes around here just love him."

We walk past trees and hanging from the limbs are colored plastic Easter eggs on ribbons. Around the bottom of the trees are circles of stuffed toy bunnies. "Look," shouts Little Lilly. "I put the bunnies a…wound (missed an r) the trees!"

Then, "He catches all kinda snakes," she continues. "Last year he filled up Grandma Lolly's bathtub with 'em. Snakes ahoy! Grandma Lolly, started boohooing when she saw them and Great Granny Blue Haired Lilac, bleeped."

I sigh… Little Lilly can talk the horns off a Billy goat.

Budgie says, "Shhhh…, Lil. Be quiet, okay? Faithy doesn't want to hear it. Besides, Doobie's partly outlaw!" I giggle. No joke.

Skeeterhawk races by, stops and yells, "Doobie ain't an

outlaw, Miss Know-It-All. He's just got a thing for snakes. He's good at snakes. Snakes like Doobie."

"But don't make Doobie mad cause he throws rocks," adds Little Lilly.

Skeeterhawk yells, "Outlaws all y 'all," and runs toward the barn.

"I never did like snakes," I say and slow down, my eyes on the barn.

It is chilly but Reader, Little Lilly, Budgie and I are wearing sweaters over our t-shirts and jeans. Plus, it will warm up. This is what spring is all about.

I have not been raised, surrounded by these country cousins at Searock City, where anything goes and seems that wild is their idea of fun. Papa says they are just different, and that they do what they want. Mama says they ARE wild. Personally, I believe they are both different and wild as they come. The word uncivilized comes to mind.

As we walk along Budgie brushes her hair with the broken brush.

"Thanks for the purty beads," Little Lilly says, fingering MY pearls on her neck.

"They're pearls," I remind her for the hundredth time.

"I can go home with you and stay a whole week when school gets out. It'll be a great adventure!" Missed a 'v'. Her long hair swings back and forth and she laughs at the thought of going home with me. Perish the thought, although I do love her.

I roll my eyes and say, "You're a good one to get those pearls. They're on loan only, okay?" I can't see her digging through my private stuff. I mean, what did I do to deserve these country cousins? Why couldn't I have cousins who are movie stars?

It is almost funny. These cousins are my blood kin. Their faces are in frames in my home back in Busted Knuckle. Busted Knuckle is not a city like say, Atlanta, Valdosta, or even Waycross, Georgia. Sure, it is small town America, but still a good way from this place here, Searock City. And Reader, I sure wish I was back at Busted Knuckle right now in my house safe and sound and chatting up Uveda on the phone!

"Faithy! Hey, hey, hey!" cry the twin cousins, Tee and Jee running toward us.   They live in one of the six houses, the one with the sign *Grease Monkey Garage*. Their papa, Uncle Buster, is a mechanic. Behind them, Doobie and Roper walk slowly. They act like they are carrying a very heavy *thing!*

 It is a big aluminum trash can. The bottom of the trash can makes a mark in the dirt. The can has a hooked lid, hooked; I don't want to be know.

I jam my tongue against my teeth and stop walking. I dig my Nikes into the sand and stop. I cross arms and prepare for battle! I am in the middle of a nightmare.

The boys stop about five feet away. They are very serious and sweating. Not good. They are breathing hard, hmmm.

Budgie sticks her hand, which feels like a knife blade, against the small of my back and pushes. I want to throttle her. My mouth drops open and my eyes feel cold as silver dollars. Like David facing Goliath, I need one of those magic slingshots or maybe a rocket launcher, ground-to-air missile or

AK-47; anything! My first "test" of the week! Will I pass it?

The trash sounds like someone beating it from the inside with a shoe. The boys huff and puff and drag it closer. The can is heavy yet seems walking on phantom feet. When Doobie and Roper stop, everyone gathers around the can, loving a good scare, no kidding. Not me. They lean toward the can. Except me, I lean backwards. I stare at the hooked lid with the pin prick holes. I am on my tiptoes. I hold my breath, afraid to breathe. Danger is inside this can. And it's noisy!

The dogs dart back and forth, barking at the trash can.

Inside the trash can sounds like a wild elephant beating back a forest, but it isn't Dumbo; no. And Reader, I am not some Dumbo either.

Inside the trash can is the monster coachwhip snake. I try not to creep out. My ticker double-clicks and I want to run. But I don't. This is all out war, time to be a brave soldier. And though I'm low on brawn, I have brains. And I must stand my ground. I am determined to outsmart not only my country cousins, but the coachwhip which might as well be an African cobra.

"Coachwhips, they live in the woods," says Budgie, brush, brush. Roper holds the trash can steady while Doobie unhooks, UNHOOKS, the lid. NO KIDDING! Here we go. Test time. Skeeterhawk slips a hunting knife from a pouch on his belt which has the letters S K E E T E R H A W K burned into the leather. He wipes off the knife on his jeans.

"Y 'all get back," says Doobie, hand on the lid. "We just gonna look at 'em. Nobody let the coachwhip get away."

Yeah right. Catch that sweet snake and put a dress on it!

Reader, they lean the can halfway over.

And that is when Skeeterhawk thwacks the can with his hunting knife. Once, twice, thrice: thwack, thwack, BIG thwack! Smart.

And the trash can is knocked over, as if in slow motion, from Doobie and Roper's hands with a thundering thud. Like a tree falling in a forest. Or a building collapsing.

"Let the bleeping thing go! Let the bleeping snake go,"

shouts Great Granny Blue Haired Lilac rolling across the yard in her wheelchair. Grandma Lolly runs toward us snapping a dish cloth.

And amid the screams, yells, cussing and stomping, the coachwhip snake does indeed GO. All of what looks to be a thousand feet of long, slippery, slimy coachwhip snake twists from the trash can. The snake hurtles itself from the can like a rope, spinning wheels, gyrating, taking off like greased lightning.

And I GO. I go one way, Budgie another, Little Lilly another. The boys go after the fast, slithering and frightened coachwhip. Great Granny Blue Haired Lilac pushes her wheelchair after the boys chasing the snake. She bleeps about a gall berry switch.

My poor imperfect heart beats ninety to nothing. I run toward the house and up the steps and inside. Slam the door. Whew! Think about calling Mama right now, fast. I'll threaten to run away from Searock City and my country cousins and their coachwhip snakes. I have passed one test without being tko'd in the process, but I could not, would not ever do anything this stupid again. Face a snake head on! No sir, and yes, I am scared. I'll see snakes for the rest of my days!

Behind the door, Roper yells, "Faithy, Faithy, I said don't go in yonder! I told you not to go in yonder!"

I was already "in yonder!' and the joke is on my cousins! I lean against the door as though barring it, hehe. I tiptoe and look out through the window. Roper dashes up the handicapped ramp on the side porch and pounds the door. Pound! Pound!

I hold the doorknob with both hands, tight, where it won't budge. I laugh. Roper rattles the doorknob. Ha. Ha, jokes on y 'all! I am safe, woo! Now, who's the Fraidy Cat? Am I smart or what? I sigh.

"Turn loose the doorknob, Faithy. It's me, Roper, let me in. Let me in," Roper shouts till he is hoarse. He seems sincere, wonder why?

Doobie joins the yelling, "Faithy, you turn the doorknob loose right now!"

I laugh nervously. I am outfoxing the boy cousins.

Skeeterhawk shouts, "If you got any smarts a 'tall, Faithy, you'll let us in yonder."

I hold on even tighter; too funny. I am here and they are out there!

Then something thunders like the voice of God. Only later did I realize it wasn't God's voice but Budgie's Future Teacher of America voice screaming, "Faithy, you open this cotton pickin' door right this minute. The dadgum coachwhip's gone in there!"

Roper yells, "Doobie saw the coachwhip slide up the wheelchair ramp and go inside, through the door. The snake is in the house!"

And that's when the doorknob came loose in my hand.

Chapter 5

The Window (or Long Drop) of Opportunity Opens

I, Faithy Jane Searock, am caught between a rock and the face of Mt. Everest. I am in Grandma Lolly's house. I am locked inside with a coachwhip snake. Repeat...I am locked inside with a snake. I repeated myself in order to calm down. Better I repeat the Lord is My Shepherd. I am starting to sweat. I am frozen and cannot move one-inch right or left. My brain is frozen, and I can't think.

I remember Grandma Lolly saying the locks in the house do not work. Little Lilly said a hobo walked in one night, ate and then left. This is the boonies, the smack-dab country, river woods of deep South Georgia. This is my Grandparents house where not only do the door locks NOT work, the doors stay open day and night. So, why's the living room door locked? Because the doorknob has come off in my hand, no kidding!

Why is it that I, Faithy, am the one locked in here with a snake I do not know where he is? Why is it not Budgie, Doobie or Roper? How come I, the city cousin is locked inside a house where doors do NOT normally lock? Me? Locked in with a coachwhip? Where is my luck? Am I doomed forever like a poor princess in a sad fairy tale? Has someone put a pox on me?

But heads up, Reader. I have zilch time to throw a pity party.

I, Faithy Jane Searock, have other fish to fry. I have a South Georgia coachwhip to outsmart, myself to find and some courage to muster in the process. Ta-daaaaaaaaa! I have a brain, if only I can find some steel spine to go with it. If only I can MOVE!

I look at my feet. I look around the room for a chair to jump onto. And to this day I swear I saw a slimy tail sticking out from under Grandma Lolly's beat up orange sofa. And Reader, the tail was moving.

So, I move.

Watch Faithy jump!

My heart flutters and my feet move like they are skates. No joke.

I fix my eyes on the tail and tiptoe around the room. I lunge down the hallway toward the safety of the guest bedroom. It is easy for me to be caught in Grandma Lolly's house with a monster snake. Easy to know my country cousins have set this trap for me. But it is not easy to believe I am doomed because I am determined more than ever to live! It is not over till it is over, papa always says, and I believe him!

If I call Papa, the snake will likely bite me before he can drive all the way down here. The snake grows in my mind. Before the volunteer fire department can possibly locate Searock City I will be dead as a door nail. The nearest SWAT team is (I am sure) out chasing ax murderers or dope dealers in Atlanta. The nearest Air Force bombers are at Moody Air Force Base out training flights.

Calling the local sheriff is like hollering for Barney Fife.

I am trapped but not stupid. I must think like a spy. I am

scared but not out of my mind. I am a good test taker, just not at taking trick tests of country cousins.

I close the door to the bedroom and pull back the curtains. My cousins gather below looking up. I shiver. I imagine the coachwhip snake slithering into the room and squeezing me like a python. Or spewing venom and putting out my eyes. I cringe. I choke back tears. I get a grip. I must think like a smart cookie.

When I think of no more Accelerated Reader or Miss Citizenship pins, or summer 4-H Camps at Rock Eagle (and I've only been once and mama went too!) or no going into 5th grade at Busted Knuckle, no more books, well, it makes me want to hunker down and come out fighting.

Tap, tap, tap, tap on the windowpane.

It is like a replay of this morning except the faces at the window now are full of fright. Jeez, Reader, it is down to the wire. This is serious canola.

The faces mouth G E T O U T! G E T O U T!

In a daze I see Budgie, Roper, Doobie, Skeeterhawk, Little

Lilly, Grandma Lolly, and across the yard, Great Granny Blue

Haired Lilac, motioning G E T O U T! For once they seem

united. For once they agree. They agree I am one hair away

from death at the hands of a monster snake. Pass or Fail, time,

NO KIDDING!

The cousins want me out of Dodge. Well, hello brains, I

do know they want me to jump out the window! Jump out a

window! My mouth drops open. But I move as fast as a note

snatched in the hall at Busted Knuckle.

I push hard, pull, push, lift the window. With muscle

power I never knew I had; I raise the window. It makes a

creak sound. I am tested by fire! I stick my head through the

window and look down. Might as well be the Empire State

Building!

No time to lose. I must jump or fly to the sky!

I am not crying because Reader, I am cold, frozen with

fear.

And I will always swear on a stack of Bibles the bedroom

door opens. I hear creaks and something slithers. I imagined the coachwhip changing into an alien. The snake becomes the Loch Ness monster! It rises on legs and hovers over me with its forked tongue. It flicks fire down on me. Or something I hate worse: mustard!

Below me swims a sea of horrified faces, cherry cheeks, greasy hair, yet arms wide open and stretching up, up! From the windowsill, looks like a hundred-foot drop. And I am suddenly Faitheeze of the Flying Trapeze! Not funny.

My window of opportunity (pun intended) is literally open.

Far below, Budgie, Roper, Doobie, Skeeterhawk and Grandma Lolly shout, "Come On! Come On! Jump, Faithy, jump!"

I throw my left leg over the windowsill. I hold onto the windowsill with both hands. I straddle the wooden sill and steady myself.

Will they catch me or let me bust my brains out?

It is test time. Pass or fail, brave or coward? Will my country cousins move aside, letting me to fall on rocks, boulders and thorns? Or glass from bottles Skeeterhawk shot off blocks? Or Doobie smashed with rocks?

A splinter sticks in my tail. I sit there numb. I try to find courage to hurtle myself from the window. Into the open arms of the dingbats who've gotten me into this mess in the first place, but it is either me and them, or me and….

A thump lobs against the bedroom door. The door opens slightly; I am here, and I hear this. I know what is taking place.

I grip the window and scream, although I'd sworn to not wimp out. It is me and my country cousins or me and a coachwhip snake. Reader, do I have a choice here?

My right tennis shoe does not touch the bedroom floor. My left foot dangles outside the window. Doobie snags my foot. He is standing on Roper's back. Budgie's arms are outstretched. She shakes her brush up at me. C O M E   O N   J U M P! They motion for me to jump! Granny Lolly mouths *Do it! Go for it!*

I look toward the bedroom door and as they say in the movies, my life at Busted Knuckle Elementary School passes before me. Left out in the clutch? Can I beat this? Arggghhhhh. I must move. I must do something!

I've heard folks say they're ready to meet their maker. They say I'm ready to go but you know what? Reader, not me! I don't want to leave this world yet. I had not asked to leave Busted Knuckle and spend a week at Searock City. I want to go home!

Thump against the door. My mind is past thinking. I am horrified in fragments. Thump. A snake is calling. Would you like to buy some perfume? Cookies?

A rebel yell forms. At the same time, Doobie yanks my foot and I jump or fall out the window like a comet. I land atop Budgie, who falls on Doobie, Tee and Jee, who squash Roper, who ka-thumps Skeeterhawk sideways. Helter Skelter comes to mind.

From the edge of the pile pokes Little Lilly's legs. She crawls away, screaming, "I am dead now. I am dead." She jumps up. "I done broke Faithy's beads. I done broke Faithy's beads! Wahhhhhhhhhh!"

"Beads? You mean pearls!" I squeal and gaze about. I get up on my all fours.

Doobie rolls over and spits out a button. Roper crawls out from under the pile and Budgie lies there still as a dead doe. My head pounds and my heart races.

Roper and Skeeterhawk jump up. They brush off their clothes and stand underneath the window. They scratch their chins, then their heads. They make a chair with their hands and boost Doobie up. With a heave-ho, Doobie grabs the windowsill and hoists himself up. He disappears through the window.

I look up and see something sort of funny.

I see the dang window is not as high up as I had thought. It is not far from the ground. I had made this leap a lot scarier than what it was. It is somehow funny now that I am on the dirt on skint knees, but not really, because I've learned something.

I've learned that my fear of jumping out the window is worse than the JUMP itself. Hello, Faithy, you **COWWWWWARD!** Yep, it is not funny.

It was not as bad as I'd thought so of course the joke is on me; always.

I sit up on the ground and Skeeterhawk's hound dog licks my knees. Budgie brushes my hair with her broken brush. Hmmm, something tells me I have trusted these country cousins way too much; way too much.

They haven't saved me after all. I have saved myself.

I take the trust back as fast as pulling wedgies. Trust is special; something folks earn. It is not something given easily like a card for birthdays or gum on a bus ride.

I am not a trust fund. If my cousins want my trust, they must earn it just like the rest of the world. And so far, Reader, nobody has earned *my* precious trust. Except me.

Y 'all may say I'm hard-headed, even hard-hearted. Y 'all may say I'm stubborn as a mule, but I am what I am. I am Faithy, a real hard egg to crack.

This coachwhip thing may have been a cousin's joke to get my goat; do me a number. To laugh about under the sheets at midnight when I am back in Busted Knuckle licking my wounds.

The cousins may joke about me around Grandma Lolly's kitchen and slap the table as they snicker behind my back. They'll make fun of me like cousins do. I can very well become the laughingstock; there's one in every family! That is the cold plain truth.

Papa would say, "Faithy, your imagination's running away with you." And I know it may be, but if I am to trust these country cousins then something real, not fake, needs to happen. Not something silly like a dumb snake; something more. More than a leap from a window I can walk out of! More than a ruse to get me to jump out of a window.

Grandma Lolly yanks Budgie up. "Stand up, Budgie, you ain't hurt."

Budgie yanks me up, "Get up Faithy. You ain't hurt."

"I am," Little Lilly cries. "I hurt Faithy's bestest beads.

Wahhhhhh!"

Doobie runs out the front door with Grandpa Liston right behind him slinging a belt. In Doobie's hands is the long, black, slime-bag coachwhip snake. Unbelievable! Doobie races past us and Roper, Skeeterhawk and Tee and Jee chase them. They disappear around the corner of the barn. I've never heard such a ruckus in my life!

Grandpa Liston comes back around the barn and takes me by the hand.

He says, "Don't worry, young'un. They promise they ain't scaring you no more. Come on now, I want to show you my birds."

I brush off my knees. They are skint and bloody. Mama will have a hissy fit when she sees (IF she sees) how banged up I am. My wounds burn me, but I wince and walk.

"What birds?" I asked, dreading to know. It is a nightmare.

"Let her rest up," says Grandma Lolly. Yes, please.

"Those birds will kill a young'un like Faithy," shouts Great

Granny Blue Haired

Lilac. Her apron is full of gall berry switches plus a can of

sweet snuff.

And at Great Granny Blue Haired Lilac's words, "birds will

kill" I do what any city slicker will do (slight heart condition

remember?). I faint dead away. Which saves the day, because

I wake up in Grandma Lolly's big 'ole feather bed. On the side

table is a cucumber sandwich and a glass of tea with mint

julep, whoever heard of such?

Somewhere between night and Easter Sunday I will get

another chance to trust one or more cousins. Which cousin,

who knows? But I feel this like a wave coming at me when I

go out too far. Yes, something is on its merry way. And since

fate never keeps a secret for very long, she speaks sooner than

later.

The next morning, as I jump out of bed, fully clothed mind

you, I know I will be slammed again because the cousins trick

war is raging, and I am "it". Reader, here, tricks are the meal

of the day! I listen for Yellow Boy's shrill *Help! Help!* I have decided the rooster crows and wakes folks up mad. And mad

folks are dangerous!

I should have stayed in bed and prayed.

Chapter 6

Who Wants to Be a Bird Bustin' Champion?

It is day two (Tuesday) of Easter week at Grandma Lolly and Grandpa Liston Searock's farm down by the Satilla River. My country cousins seem bent on picking me apart limb by limb. It is day two of my being thought of as Faithy Jane, fraidy cat, shy, wimpy, city slicker coward me. But somewhere deep inside something is going on.

Somewhere inside me, I have found something I was not seeking. I have found-er, not sure yet, what, but something and when I figure it out, I'll let you know, Reader.

No. one, I do not like being the wuss they think I am. I plan to duke it out when the next disaster strikes. I lay awake last night and re-thought the coachwhip incident. I am seeing how fear rode me hard. Mind you, fear, not the jump. Not the snake. Really, just fear. And I see how many times in my nine point five years of living, almighty fear has been worse than the "thing"! Yep, the snake was scary. But I survived the ordeal!

And Reader, I still am not real sure how one overcomes fear, but I hope to find a way. I hope to shake the shivers loose like a dog shaking off water.

Now the clan is in the kitchen around Grandma Lolly's long oak table. Budgie's broken brush sticks out the top of her shorts pocket. Little Lilly stands beside my empty chair. Around her neck are my pearls on what look like twine. Twine?

Doobie and Roper eat hotcakes and Skeeterhawk picks his teeth. Tee and Jee pour syrup on their hotcakes. In the corner Great Granny Blue Haired Lilac sleeps in her wheelchair with a cat curled up on her lap. Great Granny drools on the cat and it fights the slobber in very slow motion; fun!

"What happened to the dumb snake?" I ask, as I sit down. Little Lilly sits down on the edge of my chair and gets close to me. She is warm and thin. She is happy.

"He..." "Ah, the snake..." "The booger..." "Wow," the

boy cousins shout in unison. "Man, you shoulda seen 'em go." "Well, the snake was fast." "He was too fast for us."

"Whoa," I say, "Whoa. What happened to it?"

Grandma Lolly holds up an index finger, "Shhhh," she says, "Let Faithy eat." She smiles like yesterday's snake disaster is par for course.

The cousin's smile like yesterday is a feather in their caps. Little Lilly squeals happily like it is just more of the same.

I do not smile. Yesterday was one of the worst experiences of my life. It is and never will be funny nor a warm memory. Who do these country cousins think I am? Do I look like a total nincompoop?

"So okay, I am asking a question. Where'd the coachwhip go?" I ask and they laugh. I frown and they laugh harder and elbow each other. I purse my lips.

But nobody tells what happened to the snake. I let it slide as we finish eating and head outside. I have no choice but face day two of Easter vacation week. I have to get this over with. Mama says time is on your side, and all I can think is, let's hope it flies!

I am amazed how my cousins never watch television or stay indoors. They live life outdoors in the wild woods. They seem to love it, but Reader, so far, I sure don't. But I'll say it again, I am stuck like glue here for a few days. No kidding.

This time, Grandpa Liston leads the way. "To see the birds," he announces...

Grandpa Liston is a sight for sore eyes in overalls and a white shirt buttoned up to the neck. To me, he is a cute man. His overalls have lots of pockets. This would make a great costume for a play. But I won't tell my friends back in Busted Knuckle how my grandparents dress. They would not believe me anyhow.

Grandpa said, "I have these big birds you'll like."

I have heard how Grandpa Liston has gotten a pair of what he calls "exotic" Ostrich's. He keeps them in a large pen at the backside of the farm behind the barn and calls them names and pets them. Other people make boots and eat their meat but not

Grandpa, thank goodness.

He climbs onto a John Deere tractor with Tee and Jee riding on either side of a bush hog plow. Roper rides atop beside him. The tractor is loud and jerky.

Budgie, Doobie, Little Lilly and I dash across the field. We follow the tractor past oak trees and beneath long leaf yellow pines. High in the baby blue Georgia sky I think I see an Eagle. I am astonished. I find a feather on the ground.

I look at the feather and toward the sky and ask, "Eagle?"

"We see them all the time," Budgie answers. "They nest in those Cypress trees."

Cool. I've studied eagles in school. And although I'd never tell it, I love nature. Indeed, I am what they call a green earth person.

"And are those Venus fly traps?" I ask, pointing to a ditch. The ditch was full of what we call fly catcher plants. I've read in Science how Venus fly traps are endangered. I would sure never tell anyone they grow in these ditches like a cover crop. Someone might dig them up by the ton for flower shops in cities, but hey, here they are!

"They're everywhere out here," Budgie says proudly.
"Everywhere..."

We stop beside a field surrounded by a hog wire fence.
Inside the fence, strutting around making a mee… mee noise
are two huge strange birds. Too funny but they look sort of like
Big Bird on Sesame Street.

Grandpa Liston jumps down from the tractor and stands
beside the gate to the pen. He says, "These here birds are
ostriches. I got 'em in Florida. You can ride 'em like a horse.
Some people use their skin for boots; not me. They are pets
here."

"So, I'm seeing camels with feathers?" I joke, yep joke!

Grandpa Liston laughs and says, "Uh huh, camels with
feathers!"

"Their names are Boy and Girl," said Little Lilly. 'They
are berry pretty." (Missed a v). She laughed and I laughed. I
need to teach this girl her letters, grrrr.

Budgie grabs my arm. "They're pets, Faithy. At first

Grandpa got them to kill and eat the meat, but we made them pets and now we can't eat them."

I stick my finger into my mouth and gag. Little Lilly laughs.

The thought of eating such beautiful birds make me want to up-chuck.

"They tame as babies. We ride 'em all the time," Little Lilly says.

"I don't care if they're tame. I'm not exactly Calamity Jane," I say. "I came to Searock City to hunt Easter eggs with y 'all, not ride birds!" I cross my arms. I must stand my ground, Reader, I won't ride a bird! I simply refuse.

Budgie says, "Easter Eggs is next Sunday. Today is Tuesday, then Wednesday and so on. You have to survive this week. So, hang in there..." She trails off and takes out out her broken brush. She brushes her hair and stares at me. She is trying to stare me down, but little does she know, nobody can stare me down.

Let the whole world try. They *have* tried! I feel the

something stirring inside me and I know I have no fear of something as simple as a stare with eyes; nothing but eyes.

Mama and Papa have tried. The doctors and nurses have tried. The teachers at Busted Knuckle try all the time. They say THERE IS SOMETHING DIFFERENT ABOUT HER AND WE CAN'T PUT OUR FINGER ON IT. No kidding.

The problem is I can't put my finger on it either. I possibly have a great power or talent hidden in my soul (to withstand stares?) but so far, the answers have not knocked me upside the head. Maybe I have the power to overcome fear of the simplest things, or maybe I am catching on! Hmmmm? What am I good at, other than letters and pins?

Will I so called "find myself"? Will I say here's my mojo? Will I suddenly have a surge of courage and pass all these country cousins "tests" of living? I want to. Oh, how I want to! NO JOKE! You hear me, NO JOKE!

"There is a lot to do between now and Easter Eggs," Budgie says.

I shake my head, "Don't I know. Yeah. Hello fun!"

As I watch the ostriches run and spread their feathers and dip and swerve, I grow weak. I turn around, looking for a miracle which means, way out!

But I do not turn around in time.

Grandpa Liston swoops me up into his arms. Everybody laughs like crazy. I am kicking and waving my arms!

He carries me screaming through the gate and plops me down onto the ostrich's back. It is like putting a kid onto one of those fake horses, you know in front of some old five and dime store. Except this ain't Sandy and it moves without a dime!

The cousins go wild. Show time arrives and again, I am "it"! The bird stinks but is a lot thicker than one would think right off hand. It breathes heavily and I realize the bird is probably as scared of me as I am "it" oh whoa!

"Arggggh," I yell as the ostrich gallops in a circle. Grandpa Liston lopes beside me. He holds me on the bird's back. Only problem, there is nothing for me to hold onto, except feathers. I pluck a feather out of the bird! My mouth drops open!

I wisely quiet down so the bird will hopefully SLOW down. The bird lopes about like a Shetland pony NOT. After running in circles forever the bird stops. Grandpa Liston takes me off its back. I jump down, huffing and puffing as Grandpa Liston sticks Little Lilly onto the bird's back. I scramble for the red metal gate. Whew!

Little Lilly laughs and says, "Giddy-up hossy!"

I dart through the gate as the others cheer. I try not to act like I've just been scared (again) out of my skull. Yesterday's jump from the window was worse *before* I jumped, than after. So far, the lesson I've learned is the worst part of fear is well, fear itself, and well, here again, the fear of the ostrich ride was worse than the ride itself. I lived through it. I just passed another "test" and I am learning. Game is on.

Adventure of this sort is very new to me. So many times,

I've been sidelined while the children at school play games outside. Doctors' orders. Mama's orders. I've been left out because I "might" not be up to it. I might get hurt. I may tire out. It is like.... fear of what "might hurt me" has been holding me back, but now, I am sort of free to play with these country cousins. Bring it on, I am thinking, I just rode a bird!

I am let go and the world isn't stopping! I am living through it!

I am nine point five years old this Easter week. I am almost done with fourth grade (in a few weeks) and going into 5th grade at Busted Knuckle Elementary School in the fall. My country cousins are trying to make me into a country girl. Everybody wants me to get tough. Well, if it keeps on, I will be just that. Tough!

Yep, they are trying to make me a country girl and they are doing a dang good job. But I am past thinking straight. Their games won't work because I am on to them. And I have been on to them since before I came to visit this week. I know I have always been different from them as a man from the moon.

They have always picked at me and on me and this week if they want a showdown, they are going to get one!

"Bird Bustin's like bronc bustin' in the rodeos on television. Or mutton bustin; sometimes smaller kids ride goats at the rodeos to learn how to ride. These birds ride just not as good as goats," says Budgie. She pats my arm and smiles.

"Birds ain't nuttin' to be scared of," says Skeeterhawk.

"Well, right but remember one kicked me in the back and near 'bout paralyzed me," says Doobie. Roper, Tee and Jee laugh. I don't laugh because I don't see how this is funny.

"You's throwing rocks at it," says Roper.

"Yeah, well. It's just a bird," says Doobie. He points to the ostrich and pretends to throw a rock. Laughter rolls around.

"Birds have rights too," I argue. "You can get in jail for hurting birds." I smile. I am not Busted Knuckle's Miss Citizenship (twice) for nothing. Ha. Ha.

"Riding the bird isn't so bad now, is it?" says Budgie, "Grandpa loves us to ride the birds." She tries to brush my hair, but I jerk back my head.

I say, "Nah, it wasn't so bad, just different. But I ah, er, sort of liked it." Gag. I hated it and it grossed me out! I hope mama never finds out. Talk about mad.

"No, you don't like it," says Little Lilly. "You was about to scream ya head off."

I frown and wish Little Lilly would stay quiet. She knows more about me than I like. I wink and she winks. She says, "I knew you don't like the abenture." (Missed "v"). I have to work on her missing V's…

"Maybe we can get you in the rodeo in a few weeks, Faithy," says Doobie.

"Doing what?" I ask and cross my arms and think, fat chance.

"Riding a bird," Doobie said then runs toward a trail through the woods.

Roper and Tee and Jee chase Doobie. They are howling with laughter.

I ask, "Where to now?" and then wish I had not.

For Budgie grabs me by the arm and whispers low so

Grandpa Liston cannot hear us. "A big secret. They found some old boats. We're going on the river."

She pulls me by one hand and Little Lilly by the other. We race after the boys. The trail disappears through a stand of pines into the piney woods. I smell honeysuckle, yum.

Grandpa Liston shouts, "Y 'all get back 'fore dark."

Dark? I shudder and try to keep up. Be home 'fore dark sounds uncivilized! Kids in Busted Knuckle stay mostly indoors and never stray from our own front yards. I mean, crooks are out there! The world has changed mama says.

Now the word "river" strikes both delight and fear in me. For Reader, to this day I am fascinated as I am afraid of water. I was born under the sign of Aquarius so yes, I'm a water baby. But ponds, oceans, tubs, swimming pools terrify me. Even the bathtub scares me. Why, river is another word altogether!

Dark swirling water and no bottom you can see; just sayin'. Gives me creeps!

I've heard it all my life--the river doesn't care. It will drown you if you can't swim and then they get out those drag nets!

We run through woods thick as old clothes in a closet. We duck beneath a canopy of live oaks. The woods trail widens into a jutted hard red clay road and slopes sharply cuddled by briars. We are moving downhill where the grass is greener.

I catch the river smell. It is a wet-dog smell mingled with fish and mud. My nose knows this scent. Reader, if you've ever smelled a river the smell crawls into your very soul and you never forget it. I love it but I've said it, it scares me.

We cross over a stream on a foot log. Budgie and Little Lilly run over the foot log like squirrels. I try twice before I find my footing and tiptoe across holding my arms like a pole. Woo…, I make it to the other side!

The Satilla River is awful flooded. It is swollen, clogged with debris, limbs, twigs, logs, trees. Plain as truth, here is a disaster waiting to happen.

I shiver from both the wild beauty and cold fear. Will this be my next country cousins test, and will I pass it? My mouth is dry as we scramble down the bank.

On the riverbank are two boats bottom-side up. One is a canoe painted on its side, DOOBIE. The other is a square, army green fishing boat with a rusted motor. The top is off the motor and chunks of the old engine are gone.

Paddles are hidden beneath the boats. But to thicken this plot by leaps and bounds there are no life jackets. I repeat, NO life jackets.

"I'm not going," I vow, backing away. I am nine point five, not just born.

"I am," says Little Lilly, "riding the ribber's fun."

"But the river is flooded," I say, stuffing my hands into my pockets. There's water everywhere I look! Lots of it!

Budgie shakes the broken brush at me. "How do you expect to learn life in the country if you don't enjoy nature? You can't be satisfied just reading about it!"

I think, why I'll stay on the bank and watch. I'll wave when y 'all float by. I'll write your names in the sand if you sink! Ha. And yes, I'll write it in a book!

The boys turn the boats right-side up and carry them to the

water. Doobie, Roper, Tee and Jee and Skeeterhawk jump into the fishing boat. They sit squashed together like a peanut butter and jelly sandwich.

This leaves the canoe to me, Budgie and Little Lilly. Reader, did you read what I said? Me, Budgie and Little Lilly! Because see, my feet walk toward the canoe, zombie-like. The cousins control me! And at the same time something in me says don't be a chicken, flap, flap, flap! I do feel bolder than yesterday. And I do know that I'm doing this, sink or swim!

I know this is it, no turning back. The test to end all tests!

Doobie switches boats at the last minute; bully for Doobie.

I crawl onto the canoe's center seat. How can I not when a five-and-a-half-year-old is in the canoe waiting for me? Budgie sits behind me on the end and Doobie holds onto the front of the boat. He has a beat-up sort of chopped off paddle.

Little Lilly shouts, "Grandma Lolly says stay off the ribber 'cause it's fwooded. Stay off the ribber." (Missing an "l" as well as "v's".)

Doobie pushes away from the bank then hops into the

front. Like on a mission, the canoe floats to the center of the wide, tea colored waters of the Satilla River. Nearby, sugar white sandbars curve like question marks.

I can't see the bottom. But when I close my eyes, I see myself as a sickly child, as an A student at Busted Knuckle Elementary School, where I collect Miss Citizenship pins. I see myself working on not trusting anyone. Because everyone has let me down, like this river here, might!

But my life whizzing by is not as bad as it is going to get.

The soul of something else, more precious than gold, will pass by before this day is over. And I, Faithy Jane Searock, will become either a Great American Hero or a coward who walks away.

Chapter 7

Life or Death on the Satilla River

Many folks believe rivers are lazy places with nothing much happening. But they are the opposite. And the Satilla River, on Day Two of Easter Week, is bloated. It is overflowing, clogged and rocking like a baby cradle.

I have seen this river many times, but this is my first time ON the river. (And with my country cousins who, I am convinced are out to t-k-o me!) I am scared, true, but at the same time, Reader, I am fascinated. It is a free-for-once feeling and I am surprised to admit I love it. It is a shame I can't (won't) admit this to my cousins. But I can't give them any ammo. Remember, I, Faithy, have a trust issue as mama reminds me often.

The Satilla River, woo, what a beautiful river she is, although right now, flooded and scary. Something spiritual rides these waters; I feel it! True, I can never tell mama and papa but what am I seeing, gracious me, is alligators! One suns himself on the bank and two smaller gators cruise the river like mini submarines. Amazing.

When I spy the gators, I look around startled at Budgie. She goes SHHHHH like don't wake those boogers. I think, hello, I don't do stupid! Would I, an A student, stir up prehistoric alligators? Nope. I don't tangle with gators!

Swish., swish., swish, sounds the currents. Thud, dink, swoosh.

Slurp, slurp, slurp. The canoe knifes through the water.

Ahead, Skeeterhawk, Tee and Jee slog through the waters. The motor on their square clunker of a fishing boat does not work so they are paddling or trying.

I grip the left side of the canoe so hard my knuckles pop. I tell myself to relax. I let go of my grip on Little Lilly. She takes her arm from around my waist and begins pointing at trees, birds and clouds.

"We do this all the time," she says. "Look! Look! Bery Bootiful," (missed some letters!) She points to a great blue heron taking flight. And yes, it is beautiful!

Budgie says, "Shhhh. You scared the heron."

"But Doobie says don't y 'all tell nobody we gone on the ribber," says Little Lilly, "but he doesn't say I can't point stuff out." She points, points, points!

Budgie repeats, "Shhhh. Then why are you telling? Just point, okay?"

"Because it's fun and Faithy, she needs some fun. Grandma Lolly says, 'When Faithy comes y 'all show her what country life's all about! The ribber's country life," says Little Lilly. She fingers her (my) pearls as she chatters on and points.

"We can swim like fish," Budgie says.

"I bet," I said, "But I can't, not one lick. I, Faithy Jane Searock couldn't swim if I was offered ten million dollars, a part in a movie or sing on American Idol or, or anything.

Something bumps the canoe. The canoe tips. No kidding.

"Gators," I cry and pull Little Lilly closer.

"Nah; limb," says Doobie. He pushes the limb away with his paddle.

A turtle clings to the limb. As the limb floats downriver,

the turtle falls off with a plop and vanishes. A fish jumps over the limb. Had I not seen this; I would not believe it; too funny. Then I hear an owl hoot; odd for this time of day?

Because the Satilla River has flooded its banks, the tea colored water is hundreds of yards into the flood plain area. I know "flood plain" because I studied rivers the first half of 4th grade at school. I have been interested in science and now I am on the Satilla River firsthand. Jeez. Yow. I love it, like I said, but I can't admit this.

I gaze at the boat in front, at the backs of Roper, Skeeterhawk, and the skinny twins Tee and Jee. Although my cousins are young, they know this river. They know more than we city kids do. A part of my heart is startled by this truth, and sad I've been so left out. I've been left out so many times I have felt like an onlooker. But I am not being left out this time, I am ON the river. So here, I am happier. I am happy with this new having-fun-in-the-country feeling. But I won't admit it, to them!

In the boat, Roper paddles and Skeeterhawk steers from the

back seat. Tee and Jee sit side by side on the middle seat. Tee trails a long stick in the water and on the right side Jee tries to snag a board. Something will bite your hand off, I think.

Surprisingly enough, I am more relaxed than before we came out on the river. Again, the fear of getting ON the river had been greater than the "thing" itself. As Doobie paddles the canoe, his arms move like a windmill turning on a breeze.

The eyes in the back of my head see Budgie smiling at me, a teacher-type smile of approval. Budgie says she will be a teacher someday. About now I figured she is thinking of me as a slow learner finally catching on!

Limbs, twigs and trees drift by and the muddy water bears plastic dishes and a chair. Could this be from a house? My nostrils itch.

Our canoe snags the chair. Doobie pushes the chair away which tips the canoe. Whoa! I wince. I am not a swimmer! And I have zilch desire to swim with gators, even if I could. I love this though, not telling it!

How my cousins have hoodwinked me into crawling into

an old canoe and floating down a river I don't know. How they lived such uncivilized lives I don't know. They remind me of wild horses running free. Is this country life good or bad? IDK.!

Then like a lightning bolt from a clear sky something happens which makes me know about trust and freedom, something which takes some time to unravel because it changes my life. Reader, my thinking gets an overhaul.

Try to understand again why I feel like I do. I am considered frail (heart murmur) though I feel wiser than most. I read a lot and if you read tons of books you get brainy. I am also wiser than my years because of doctors. Now, here I am a flat-out genius!

I've seen more doctors in my nine point five than all my friends crammed together.

A heart murmur is an interesting ailment. For example, sometimes I have zilch energy compared to Billy Joe Weber at school. They dose Billy Joe up to keep him nailed to his seat, while the teacher drills us on the Colonies, geography and continents of the world. So really, if I have less energy than a dosed-up kid, then Reader, I have NO energy at all.

One of the doctors says my heart ailment can TKO me anytime. Another doctor says many people have this and I will live to a ripe old age. The first doctor says this means about 11 years ripe. The second doctor says hogwash, more like 100!

Mama agrees with the first doctor; it being her nature to see the worst. (Why she is on me like a guard dog 24/7). I mean. she hovers like a life-flight helicopter.

Papa agrees with the second doctor who disagrees with the first. Papa says I will be fine, "Go on and run the 100-yard dash if you want to!" But since he and Mama disagree, and she always wins I am grounded for life (or have been!)

But my great trickster Papa always has an ace up his long sleeve banker's shirt.

And Papa has Grandma Lolly and Grandpa Liston on his side. They say they prayed for me and God Almighty says I will be alright. That God says let me go and live life, for crying out loud. Grandpa Liston, with his long face and twinkling brown eyes, says many times, "Teach Faithy blind faith and to look up and never down. She is to overcome and get her mojo going'!" I love my grandpa's attitude, always have!

So, although I go with the blind faith theory and getting my mojo going, fear is a hard thing to shake loose. But 'm determined and here, I'm on my way.

I have no choice. Grandpa says when people give up they are done for.

Grandma Lolly says, "Man says one thing, God says another!"

I want to be A-Okay. If it means eating liver and choking on spinach or boating down a river with country cousins, fine! Give me life! I think about my favorite saying by the blind lady Helen Keller: "Life is either a daring adventure or nothing." (And Reader, write this down and pin it to your bulletin board so you too will always be inspired!) It's a great thought and I love it.

But courage and trust have not come easy. With endless

white nurse uniforms, plus my parents and family pulling in opposite directions, who can a nine point five believe? It has been confusion yes it has!

The only good side is this...If I am nervous about in general living, then this trip down the Satilla River is a piece of cake. I mean, this is easy. I am floating down the Satilla River in a canoe. There is nothing out here but white and blue herons and jumping fish, rocking brown water and turtles on limbs. The sky above is baby blue and the sunshine warms me. My nose loves the smell of wet-dogs and craw daddies. Oh, and the alligators. Whoo, they are fierce! Scary but amazing.

But on this, day two of Easter Week, I find out destiny has other plans like she always does. Sow one seed, relax, and reap another seed. Terror is straight ahead!

Yep, destiny says it is high time I, Faithy, learn a lesson about trust.

But it isn't only me; no. It is Budgie, Doobie, Roper, Skeeterhawk, Little Lilly, Tee and Jee, plus something that's never laid eyes on a human being.

And a river which refuses to let go.

Chapter 8

The Surprise Rebel with a Cause

I see the blue barrel with a white stripe floating in the river.

The fishing boat carrying Roper, Skeeterhawk, Tee and Jee floats past the barrel. Our canoe is almost past it as we paddle around a bend. The river narrows here, and the water is colored dark brown and eddying deep, angry and fast. Overhead the sky has turned stormy blue with fluffy moving clouds. I mean, those clouds are flat our hauling buddy!

The blue barrel is caught in limbs at the edge of the bank and a river wash. There is no lid on the barrel which rocks from side to side. Water slaps the metal and the sound is like a pounding on the back. Like at Grandpa's church praying for sinners. No let up whatsoever! Slap, slap, slap!

I hear the sound first; a sound inside the barrel. It is a high-pitched cry for mercy, and it is flat out pitiful! No kidding. The sound is real, real pitiful.

"Oh!" I cry as though stung. My mouth pops open and my

eyes stretch.

"What's that?" Little Lilly asks, scooting closer to me and wrapping her left arm around my waist. From the barrel comes the cry again—baby or animal?

Behind me, Budgie says, "Shhhh...Doobie, go closer. Take us close!"

In the fishing boat Roper and Skeeterhawk drag their paddles in the water. They try to stop and turn the fishing boat, but they fight strong currents.

"Stop man!" yells Roper. He twists on his seat and motions to Skeeterhawk, who digs his paddle, trying to guide the boat towards the barrel.

"Oh! Hurry," I beg. I am alarmed and my heart goes butta-butta-butta!

Doobie gets there first and our canoe bangs against the blue metal barrel and bounces away. Again, Doobie lurches toward the barrel. Again, a high-pitched cry comes from inside the barrel. I gasp. Little Lilly cries softly. Budgie says, "Shhhh, y 'all hush!" We are all wide eyed and slapping yellow flies.

"Hurry," yells Skeeterhawk. "Get there."

"It's a baby in there!" cries Little Lilly.

"Shhhh," says Budgie. "We don't know what's in there."

"It's something," I cry, "but not a baby." My mouth is dry as cotton. My eyes burn and my chest aches. It is amazing how both fire and ice race through my blood at the same time. It is amazing how I am in rescue mode!

Doobie wrestles with our canoe against the current. Budgie digs in with a limb and the canoe shoots toward the barrel. Doobie swings sideways against the barrel and brings the center of the canoe to the mouth of the drum.

Where my seat is, where I sit, is at the center of the canoe. So, I Faithy, am centered on the floating barrel filled with cries for mercy. I am "the one" …no kidding.

An alligator bellows downriver. The foghorn sound reminds me I am not alone in this world, nor meant to be. I am not an island. I am on a team here, and I am here to do my part. I smell fish and think it smells rotten. I wonder if death or half-death is in the barrel. And I know I am going to find

Faithy · 91

out.

The high-pitched meee-meeee comes again and we stare at the barrel and at each other...All of us are afraid. Afraid something alien will pop out any minute. (Yep, I watch too many scary movies!) And also afraid for whatever is making those cries.

I cry, "Oh," and Little Lilly cries louder.

Beside me, on her hands and knees in the bottom of the canoe, Budgie says, "Shhhh!"

Doobie says, "Y 'all hush!"

Every time I moan, "Oh my!" and every time Little Lilly sobs, the wail for mercy answers. And a fire lights my soul! And for this reason: I recognize the sound coming from the barrel. Because Reader, I've heard it stuck in my own craw.

The sound is the cold and lonely sound of fear.

It is the sound of *I'm all alone, left out, orphaned.* It was the sound of, *what now? What do I do next? Where do I go? Who do I turn to? Who will save me?*

The pitiful cry echoes against the canoe and boomerangs

off the wall of oaks and pines and water. The canoe floats inches away then Doobie pushes the paddle deep and the canoe pops back with a thud. Bang. Back again, slosh, slosh, bang, bang.

Tears fill my eyes. Beside me, Budgie wipes her eyes. Little Lilly sobs until she has hiccups. She moans.

"Please, get it fast!" I cry. I hear courage. I am proud. I hear my mojo. I feel my blind faith. I know why my name is Faithy! I know what I came to do!

"Catch it, catch it!" I beg. My spine stiffens as a strange breeze from nowhere swooshes me with power. I suck in my breath and square my shoulders.

I hear a voice, "I am the spirit of courage, Faithy. And I give courage like the roar of the river, to you girl. You are well now and free. Free to be the Faithy you were born to be." The whisper fades and like a window to my soul which has been dark I am filled with light.

"Catch the edge!" I yell. Doobie steadies the canoe. I lean over the side of the canoe. I stretch; it's too far. No good. I reach again. I stretch over the gap of angry river water and the blue metal barrel with its white stripe.

"Budgie, hold the canoe steady," Doobie shouts. Budgie grabs hold of the limbs of a tree. The tree hunches over the river like an old man carrying goods on his back. She holds the canoe snug against the barrel. The barrel bangs against the side of the canoe.

Doobie inches to the center of the canoe and leans over the side. He catches the barrel at the top and holds tight. He grunts. A yellow fly lands on his neck and he wiggles. Little Lilly stands up and leans and slaps the yellow fly, nearly knocking Doobie off the boat.

Roper and Skeeterhawk guide the fishing boat to the crook of the wash and wedge it against a pair of cypress knees. The back of the fishing boat pushes against the barrel. The fishing boat is longwise beside the barrel. The canoe is perpendicular.

If the barrel tears away, it will float downriver, carrying the trapped animal to death.

Inside me, the voice is like a ringtone, "Faithy! Faithy

Jane! Be bold. Go," And as surely as Dew covers Dixie, I whisper, "I will go!" I feel a gush of power!

I, Faithy Jane Searock, am suddenly a rebel with a cause!

"I'm getting into the barrel," I shout. I swallow a lump. I move to the left till I am face to face with the mouth the barrel. I lean over the side of the canoe. The canoe tips as I grab the sides of the barrel. The rocking barrel bumps me loose and I almost fall into the river. I grab for the white stripe.

"Hold the canoe!" I shout. I grab again. I scramble and kick.

Doobie re-steadies the canoe and Budgie holds the tree limbs. She grunts a couple of Great Granny Blue Haired Lilac's bleeps. Little Lilly sobs. In the other boat Roper and Skeeterhawk, Tee and Jee slap yellow flies and yell instructions.

The barrel rocks against the canoe, tree, bank and river wash. The fishing boat knocks against the barrel, and the river wash slaps against both boats. Water sloshes into the canoe and covers my tennis shoes.

I stick my head into the barrel. I suck in my breath.
Reader, talk about stinking? My stomach churns but I'm
skinny so can hold my breath for a long time.

At first, I see nothing. Then I make out this tiny ball of
spots at the bottom. My mouth drops open and I yell, "It's a
kitten! It's a baby kitten!" Oh cripes, No!

I can't reach the kitten. So, I very slowly slide over the
side of the canoe. I balance on my stomach and inch halfway
into the barrel. I huff and I puff. This is a JOB.

I cry but not too loud. Little Lilly yells, "I gotcha tennis
shoes, I gotcha tennis shoes!" My legs and knees hurt. Budgie
must have turned the tree loose because I feel her hands raking
up and down my slippery legs, trying to hang on to me. She
scratches me but doesn't let go.

And Reader, I dive headfirst into the blue barrel! Yow.

I grab the tiny ball of fur and the tiny ball of fur grabs me.

The pain is acute. I scream but do not let go. The kitten
cries but does not let go. It can't. I've got it. Budgie yells,
"Hurry, hurry, we're sinking!" The barrel twists and bobs

dangerously. The slap of water against the barrel bangs my brains.

"Pull!" I yell. "Pull me out! Get me! Get Me!"

And Doobie and Budgie pull me and the kitten free.

Doobie, who had turned loose the barrel to help pull me free, yanks off one of my Nike's and yanks so hard he falls backwards over the side of the canoe. Into the river! "Save Doobie!" Little Lilly shouts, "He's fell in! He's fell in the ribber!"

Roper swings the nose of the fishing boat around. He snags Doobie like scooping a fish into a dip net. Doobie catches hold of the paddle as Roper "fishes" him toward us.

Just then, the barrel tears free and floats out into the river, then disappears around the bend. Just like that. Everything fell in the blink of an eye.

Since Roper is "fishing" Doobie through the current this leaves me (with a tiny fireball drawing blood), Budgie and Little Lilly alone in the canoe, crying and yelling.

The fishing boat floats our way dragging Doobie through

the water. It crashes into us with a bang. The thud echoes from the forest like a baritone voice over.

And Reader, Budgie, Little Lilly and I join Doobie in the Satilla River. We fall in head-first, asking for drowning!

Just like in the movies.

Chapter 9

The River Tribe Satilla

We are shoulder deep in the Satilla River. The current is fast and mad thanks to the flooding. Little Lilly is on Doobie's shoulders (thanks to Doobie's fast thinking) and she is soaked and squalling, yelling, "I fell in the ribber, I fell in the ribber!"

The canoe hasn't gone completely over but is full of water. The fishing boat had not gone over so Skeeterhawk, Roper, Tee and Jee are already scrambling up onto the riverbank. Led by Skeeterhawk, they form a human ladder down into the water.

"Hold on, we'll get you out," yells Roper, flexing his skinny arms. I am crying but softly. I am shivering.

"Stay put," shouts Skeeterhawk, likewise flexing his and sloshing into the river. Like I can do anything else!

Skeeterhawk fights the current and yells to Roper, Tee and Jee, "Hold me, men. Tee, you hold onto that stump." Skeeterhawk moves quickly.

"We gotcha," yells Roper. Tee braces himself against a stump. "Yo!"

"We need something," says Jee. He grabs a paddle from the boat and passes it to Skeeterhawk. Skeeterhawk digs the paddle into the water trying to find the bottom. But the paddle won't dig. Skeeterhawk tosses it up onto the bank.

Now Reader, when the canoe tipped over, I had just rocketed out of the barrel. I kept holding onto the ball of fur (wrapped tightly around my hand and wrist) with claws like three-inch nails! Which I still held! And I mean tight!

We had all gone under, then miraculously surfaced and I felt like I'd been scooped out of the water by cupped hands!

Doobie had acted fast, snatching Little Lilly out of the river and popping her onto his shoulders.

Now I blew into the kitten's mouth between bouts of spitting upriver water myself; yep, I did this. Water spurted from the kitten's mouth as I held it high. We dog paddled, splashing and yelling. My legs felt like lead, but I stayed afloat, surprising me. I worked it friends, I worked it. My life depended on it!

Now Budgie choked and sputtered, and I think I heard her swear she hates Doobie and rivers and drowning. She also muttered a loon was crying! At least I think this is what I see and hear, all of it became a blur.

It was a miracle. For despite the fact we were fighting the river and trying to keep from drowning--jury still out on whether we drowned or not--I was thrilled to have saved a kitten! I was a hero! The kitten was alive, I was alive,

Doobie, Little Lilly and Budgie were alive! We were still in danger, in the river but alive and fighting!

I felt courageous because I had done something without thinking, without fear. I had acted, rather than reacted.

My hand hurt like the devil as I held the kitten high. Blood streaked down my arm from my wrist. The kitten clung to my wrist, fingers and palm. It said, "meeeee, meeee!"

The kitten was oh so tiny but seemed strong! No telling how long the almost newborn was in the barrel. What meanness was in the world to cause someone to throw a kitten into a barrel in the river. Then again, perhaps it fell in by accident. I will never know how it got into that blue barrel, but I will always know how it got out!

My feet sucked at the muddy, murky river bottom. None of us could move and the river would not let go.

So, we were not dead but Reader, we had to get to the riverbank, or we would be dead. The water was up to my neck and I struggled against the current. It knocked me but not over. It slammed me but not down.

I shuddered to think what would've happened had we turned the canoe over mid-river. There would have been five funerals: Doobie's, mine, Budgie's, Little Lilly's and one kitten. Five to bury in pine boxes like they do.

Now Doobie yelled, "Get to the bank! Hurry! I see a gator!" He points like crazy with his index finger.

Little Lilly held Doobie's ears. She looked like a drowned rat. She yelled, "We fell in the ribber. We fell in the ribber! We gonna get a tail whooping!"

Budgie yelled, "I see a gator too, hurry!" She slogged a

few feet toward the bank, pulled by Skeeterhawk. I tried to jerk my feet from the muck. Might as well be in quicksand! I could not budge, still dog paddling with one hand in the air.

"This kitten's killing me," I cried. I wondered if I would faint and drown? Before it happened, I decided, I'd toss the kitten to the riverbank.

The thought comforted me, and I squared my shoulders.

I came to Easter Week to visit my cousins, feeling afraid. Now here I am, Faithy Jane Searock, a rebel with a cause! And although I can never tell it I have somehow been set free of a grip of fear which dogged me forever. If I wasn't trapped and near drowning in the Satilla River I would weep for joy.

I slog a few feet. My feet go suuuuuucccccccccccccckkkkk.

Skeeterhawk is at the end of the human stick. He stands chest deep in the water. He holds his hand out to Budgie who is closest. In turn, Budgie stretches her right hand out to my left. I take it and our hands slip. She wraps her fingers through mine and holds on tight. She pulls me a few inches. I float backwards, still holding the kitten above me. I swallow river water and cough. I am lightheaded. I am crazy.

Reader, a time or two I almost went down. And then something like a hand cradled me again and again, pushing me up from the water and closer to the riverbank.

I stood up and Budgie yanked.

And like reeling in the catch of the day we were pulled through the river to the bank. I kept my hand in the air and moaned. Little Lilly cried. The kitten screamed, Mee Mee Meee. A jaw of life could not have pried the kitten loose.

I stumbled onto the riverbank and lay on my back. Tee and Jee yelled, "Leeches!" They pulled, knocked and beat leeches from mine and Budgie's legs. Budgie was beside me. We moaned and whimpered. I looked on in a daze as the blood suckers were peeled off my legs.

Where were my tennis shoes? I had on one sock and my right foot was gashed in three places. Plus, the leech bites. Reader, I was ready for ICU!

Doobie crawled up the riverbank and Little Lilly hopped off his shoulders. She ran to me and kicked the growing pile of leeches. She cried, "Leave Faithy alone. Leave Faithy and go back to the ribber 'ole leeches!"

"We're not bleeding to death," said Budgie. She wiped her legs and mine with leaves. The kitten on my arm looked like a rat. Blood streamed down my arm.

"Well," I said, "I for one *am* bleeding to death!" I bent my numb arm and held the cat to my stomach.

The pitiful kitten mewed softly.

Budgie sighed and said, "Dang!"

Doobie said, "Horse manure!"

Roper said, "We gotta dry off. We're gone catch trouble." The boys took off their wet shirts. They wave them around and draped them over some bushes.

We tried to soak up the sun. Then Skeeterhawk, Tee and Jee pulled the fishing boat and canoe (half sunk) onto the riverbank and turned them upside down.

"I can't believe what happened," I said. "We could all be dead."

"We fell in the ribber," said Little Lilly. "We fell in the

ribber!'

"Yeah, close call," said Roper. "Too close."

"We have to get this kitten off my hand," I said. Yet I clutched the weak kitten to me. The kitten whimpered. It is limp. But like me, hanging in there.

Budgie and Little Lilly stared at the kitten but didn't dare touch it. My ripped and blood caked arm was something even little kids understood.

All of us were exhausted, soaked, bleeding. Water-logged takes on new meaning. I was beyond wet. Overhead the Georgia sky is now the blue of a crab's claw.

Skeeterhawk threw a knife at an oak tree, going after it, throwing it again. I'd like to learn knife throwing, I think and smile.

For a while, the only sound is the kitten whining and the thud of Skeeterhawk's knife hitting the tree like exclamation points. Now and then someone spit up some river water.

There was no wind and it was odd because when I was rescuing the kitten, I will always swear I felt a gust of wind at my back. Hands scooping us out of the river!

Little Lilly moaned and Budgie grunted.

I winced, "Ya'll. I've got to get this kitten off me."

"Yeah, you've got to put something on your hand," said Budgie. "But we've got us a little problem." She began drawing in the red clay river dirt with a rock.

"What problem?" I asked. "I'm about bled to death."

"We'll get killed is what," says Doobie. "We'll catch it for real!"

"We fell in the ribber. We ain't s'posed to go out in them boats," said Little Lilly.

"That's right," said Doobie, "but who's telling?"

"Doobie's right. Who's telling?" said Budgie.

All of them looked at me. Budgie, Doobie, Roper, Tee, Jee, Little Lilly and Skeeterhawk (who stopped throwing knives) tried to stare me down. They gave me the look. And Reader--like I've said before--I'm some dumb, but not all dumb.

I was passing this test, somehow, someway, watch me

PASS THIS TEST!

"Great Granny Blue Haired Lilac has them gall berry switches," said Little Lilly. "She's gonna say, 'I'm gone whoop them young'uns tails till they purple.'" Little Lilly began to cry and added, "I don't want no purple tail!"

Budgie patted her arm and said, "Shhhh now. The whooping business was about the coachwhip snake."

"Yeah, Great Granny don't know about the river," Roper said.

"But she means it about everything. We'll be in big trouble if they find out we went out on the river. And it bad flooded," said Doobie, frowning.

"We go out on the ribber all the time. The ribber ours," said Little Lilly. "Ain't it Doobie? Ain't the ribber ours?"

"Yep," said Doobie. "It was given us by God."

"To take care of and not pa-pa-woot!" said Little Lilly.

"So how can we get in trouble?" I asked. "The word is P-O-L-L-U-T-E, pollute."

"Because grownups don't think kids should go out on the

river none of the time," says Budgie. "They think we're babies. So, we do things...ah...differently here in the backwoods, sorta undercover." Not saying we should disobey our parents, they likely know best, but if we have any fun, we have to well, have fun! We have to do things!

The cousins nodded. Yeah, yeah, and yeah!

"And one thing is we don't snitch on each other," said Roper. The cousins shook their heads, no, no and no!

"Never," said Tee. "No matter what, nobody tells on nobody."

"Never," echoed Jee. Never, never and never!

"Nebber," said Little Lilly. "Great Granny Blue Haired Lilac says," she began and just as she opened her mouth a tiny red-eye fish jumped out of her shirt pocket and landed on the side of her nose. Everybody cracked up. Doobie grabbed the red-eye and tossed it back into the river. Plink.

The laughter continued. Doobie, Tee, Jee and Roper rolled around on the riverbank. Budgie laughed till she fell off a log she was sitting on, then hugged it like a pillow. Skeeterhawk chuckled while throwing his knife. Ha, ha. Thud. Ha, ha. Thud.

I giggled and clutched the kitten. Little Lilly was the only one not laughing. She sat beside me and whimpered. She wanted to touch the kitten but as I said earlier, she knew better. She pointed to the kitten and frowned, pointed, frowned, and pointed.

The cousins stopped laughing and gathered around me.

"Okay, gang. Here's what we have to do," started Budgie.

"First off, nobody tell we went on the river," said Doobie.

"Much less fell in and almost drowned," added Budgie.

They looked at me and I nodded.

"What else?" I asked. "Don't think I'm a snitch? I'm not a snitch?" Well, I sure can't tell Mama and Papa. Mama would lock me in my room for the rest of my life.

And I didn't dare tell Great Granny Blue Haired Lilac who ruled with an iron fist, and gall berry switches. She'd set off Grandma Lolly who would set off Grandpa Liston.

Talk about a tail whooping! We'd be sore for a month, grounded for life.

Easter week is only on Day two. We had five days to go. I did not know what waited, but I had a half-starved kitten hooked to my hand. We had to get if off and find it some food. I had risked life and limb to save this kitten and now my cousins and I do something. We make a pact. I hoped I didn't have to bleed anymore.

Budgie explained, "We have to make a pact." No joke.

"Words are not enough," said Doobie. Who knew?

"What is?" I asked again. "What is NOT enough? Again, I'm not a snitch!"

"Noooo. We aren't saying you'll tattle. We just have to know. We must make a pact. We must agree. Once you tattle to grown-ups the fun stops. Living in the country is fun. But not if you let them know what's going on. We gotta stick together," said Budgie.

"Okay," Doobie said standing up and rubbing his chin.

We stood up. I wobbled and Little Lilly reached out to pet the kitten, then drew back wide-eyed when I shook my head. "You want a blood bath?"

"We have to go in," said Budgie. "First, form a circle, hold hands."

I could only hold my left one to Little Lilly so Budgie held my right elbow.

"River Tribe Satilla is what we call ourselves," said Budgie proudly. Ah.

"Faithy, we accept you into the tribe," said Doobie. The others nodded.

Yow and woo. I stood tall. This was the first club I've been invited into. It had been like everybody at Busted Knuckle Elementary was put off by my presence. They knew about my heart trouble and seemed afraid.

Not now. This was a club, cool, a tribe. Like it or not, all of us together just passed a test. This was not fake, Reader, it was real. A real-life adventure, near misses and misses and a few bulls eyes! How life is; win some lose some, but here now, we'd won a few. I know I had.

Here I was accepted! Why, this was better than Miss Citizenship pins, but I wouldn't say better than Accelerated Reader. I'll stand by books any day.

I felt proud as Budgie smeared my left shoulder with river mud. She said, "River rider is your tribal name."

"No," said Doobie. "Faithy's name is Faithy Jane Sea ROCKER!"

Budgie sighed and said, "Our sign is: touch hands back to

back. Flip over and catch thumbs. Swing the hand around and slide off the thumbs then high-five!"

I could only use my left hand. I tried it but it wouldn't work! "I can't do it. I can do it with my right when I get the kitten off," I swore. "I'm a fast learner. This sign will be a walk in the park." They all nodded.

Doobie said, "You can't tell what we do, especially if we have any close calls."

I agreed. Everybody nodded.

And then we walked along the river finally ducking beneath an old wooden river bridge. We popped up onto the red clay river road on the other side of the bridge.

We shuffled forward, silent, weary beyond words.

But whoa! A surprise awaited us! And how! On the far side of the bridge was Great Granny Blue Haired Lilac bleeping under her breath. And she was alone.

We ran to where she was, all talking at once, our eyes popped out of our skulls at the sight of Great Granny Blue Haired Lilac sitting there. At the same time, Grandma Lolly and Grandpa Liston rushed from the river woods towards us.

They were yelling. This was not good.

We cousins stared at each other, at the kitten, back at her.
My eyes were popped out like the front end of a Volkswagon
Bug. I could feel them about to shoot forth like one of those
rolled up whistles you blow or like marshmallows on a stick!
And Great Granny Blue Haired Lilac leaned over to me and
whispered, "Gimme the lynx!"

Chapter 10

The Kitten That Is Not a Kitten

Picture this.

Eight of us had popped up from underneath an old wooden bridge. The kitten clung to my right bloody hand. Mine and Budgie's legs were scratched, and blood streaked from leech bites. My shoes were missing, and I had on one sock.

Our clothes were caked with red river mud and Budgie's sleeve was ripped off. Talk about the Walking Dead!

Little Lilly's pants were shredded. Doobie moved like sleep walking; his thick hair plastered to his head. Reader, we looked like we'd been in a chicken fight.

We were a right sorry looking bunch and the last thing on earth we needed to see right then was Great Granny Blue Haired Lilac. I mean, how did she get there?

Had her wheelchair somehow sprouted wings? Was she Super

Great Granny? How in the ham-sam had she gotten there?

"Jesus Christ!" whispered Doobie. He stopped and I ran into his back. I put my head down and butted him to keep from smashing the kitten. He grunted.

"Ut-oh!" exclaimed Skeeterhawk. He walked ahead of us beside Tee and Jee.

"If it ain't Great Granny," whispered Budgie. She kept walking although slower. She looked back and snarled, "Don't stop! Don't let on!"

And we tried our best to NOT LET ON about the river accident for which we'd be grounded for life. Or arrested for disobeying our parents. Or sent to boot camp for juvenile delinquents to dig deep holes.

But Great Granny Blue Haired Lilac, who often said, *I was born at night but not last night*, is nobody's fool. She stared with her evil eye. To me, she was a monarch in a wheel chariot. I could not look her in the face, if I did, she would KNOW.

I felt weak but not faintly weak from fear, just weary weak.

Little Lilly clung to my left hand and said, "We gonna get our tails whooped. She's got them gall berry switches." She refused to walk another step.

"Shhhh," said Budgie. She knelt before Lilly and pushed Lil's long wet hair from her face. "Now 'member, don't tell what happened back yonder. You don't want to tattle, do you? You want friends, don't you?"

Little Lilly snubbed, "No! No! I don't wanna tattle-tail and I want bestest friends!"

Budgie said, "Okay, good. Don't say word one, you hear?"

Budgie stood and said, "Come on." And we walked toward the guillotine, er, wheelchair, toward Judge Great Granny.

We inched like worms. Great Granny Blue Haired Lilac muttered under her breath. And that's when Grandma Lolly and Grandpa Liston raced like madmen from the woods, yelling bloody murder.

"Lilac, you scared the bee-Jesus out of us! How did you get down here?" Grandma Lolly yelled as she reached the wheelchair. Grandpa Liston put his hands on the wheelchair handles and whisked it around. He said, "Whew! Scared us to death!'

"Who brought you down here?" Grandpa Liston demanded. "I'm gone tan somebody's hide! You had us ready to call the Sheriff!"

We girls reached the wheelchair. Skeeterhawk, Roper, Tee and Jee ran down the river road. Budgie walked around the chair, pulling Little Lilly by the hand. Nobody said word one. We are too scared to talk!

Dummy me. I was exhausted yet fascinated how a human being of this age could get through these Georgia woods to the bridge without anyone seeing. Suddenly, Great Granny Blue Haired Lilac became a hero like the blind woman named Helen Keller.

I stopped. Grandpa Liston works the wheelchair up and over a muddy red clay rut. Grandpa Liston and Grandma Lolly knelt beside the wheelchair and fussed over the stuck wheels.

Grandma Lolly said, "Liston, this is nuts."

The kitten screams.

They looked at me and for the first time at the kitten. Great Granny Blue Haired Lilac says, "Leave them bleeping young'uns alone. They ain't done nuttin'." But Grandma Lolly jumps to her feet and yells, "Boys, y 'all come back here right this minute. Y 'all come back here. I mean it!"

Budgie, Little Lilly, Skeeterhawk, Doobie, Roper, Tee and Jee froze on the narrow red clay river road; stopped in their tracks. From the backside they looked like statues on a town square. Their clothes stuck to them like glue. They did not turn around. I thought, ha, they are some dumb, but not plumb dumb. I almost cried, thinking, we cousins, are about to get it. No joke. Not just me, them too. Will we pass this test?

Grandma Lolly shouted, "Young 'uns! Have y 'all been in swimming? Have you? Have you?"

"They better not be," said Grandpa Liston, arms crossed.

Great Granny Blue Haired Lilac said, "I'll whoop 'em till they turn purple." She spat tobacco juice into the weeds.

"I asked a question and I want an answer," shouted Grandma Lolly. Little Lilly began to sob but did not turn around. "Have y 'all been in swimming?"

And Budgie, Doobie, Roper, Skeeterhawk, Tee and Jee

yelled in unison loud enough to crack glass, No, no and then a

big NOOOOOOOOOOOOOOOOOOOOOOOOO!" The echo

of the *NO* banged against the Pines, Tupelos, Blackjack Oaks

and Cypress trees like when a word is so great it lassos you.

The no did just that. It lassoed us, like a hangman's noose.

Grandma Lolly's mouth dropped open as the boys walked

on. She harrumped and snorted like a mad horse!

Grandpa Liston unstuck Great Granny Blue Haired Lilac's

wheelchair and rolled her down the red clay river road.

Grandma Lolly walked beside the chair on the left and I

walked on the right. They walked quietly, which means things

are not good. I mean, not good, not good and Not Good!

But I felt proud walking beside a wheelchair carrying my

great granny who was old as the green Georgia hills. I realized

that her spirit is in me, her genes, and I liked this a lot. And

Great Granny Blue Haired Lilac must have felt the same

because she smiled and shouted, "If they done something

wrong, they have to be punished but in the right way."

Grandma Lolly and Grandpa Liston look at each other stunned. She was the one who was always wanting to make the children mind. She was the tough one.

And it was at this point in this great adventure, that Great Granny Blue Haired Lilac's eyes twinkled, and remember, she leaned over and whispered, "Gimme the lynx!"

Up until this moment I thought the grownups had not noticed the kitten. But I should have known Great Granny Blue Haired Lilac had not missed a beat.

Grandma Lolly and Grandpa Liston stopped. They moved closer to me and stared. "Good grief, Faithy. You're bleeding!" said Grandma Lolly. "We have to get you home and doctor those scratches! Do they hurt? My stars Liston! Look at her!"

"And her legs," said Grandpa Liston. "She's been eaten up by leeches!"

"She'll be alright," declared Great Granny Blue Haired Lilac.

I took the kitten from my waist and handed it to Great Granny Blue Haired Lilac. She grabbed it firmly but gently and poked it into her apron pocket and patted it on the head. Then she took a bottle of water from her apron and wet her fingers and stuck them into the pocket.

"It's alright now," she said smiling. "I always wanted me one of them. Give me a day or two. You kids won't believe this thing."

"What's a lynx?" I asked and stare at the tiny head of wet fur peeking from Great Granny Blue Haired Lilac's pocket. "I thought it was a kitten."

"I was about to ask you," said Grandma Lolly, "where you found this...this lynx?"

"We ah, er, got it in the woods, down by the river," I say. "A barrel floated to the edge and we pulled it out, or, er, I did." I mean, this much was true.

"Well, it's not a kitty," mumbled Great Granny Blue Haired Lilac. "I had yawl's Uncle Theron ride me on the wagon through the woods to the bridge. He was on the tractor pulling hay to the pasture and seen y 'all go to the river. I knew you'd come up at the bridge because Theron's dog followed the trail. Just put his nose to the dirt and trailed ya, and this ain't a kitty, Faithy. This here's is a N 'danger lynx!"

"Endangered animal?" Granny Lolly said.

Grandma Lolly and Grandpa Liston pushed Great Granny's wheelchair.

A John Deere tractor drove onto the road from a side trail and Uncle Theron jumped down. The tractor pulled a hay wagon.

"Hey Theron, help us," said Grandpa Liston. "Y 'all gonna worry me to death."

"Well, I brought her out here and left her. It's what she said do. And here I am back to fetch the old gal home," Uncle Theron said, laughing.

Grandpa Liston says, "Well, I've asked you not to do stuff like this. And I sure don't see it's all so funny." But he and Uncle Theron lifted Great Granny Blue Haired Lilac's wheelchair onto the wagon. They brace her with two bales of hay. Grandma Lolly and Grandpa Liston jumped on. We everyone jumped onto the wagon, even the boys.

We rode about a country mile along the red clay road. We passed the houses on Searock City river road and puttered through the piney woods to the big house.

We ran inside for baths, for supper and trying to dodge grownups like the plague. It didn't work because charm wears off fast.

"I'll call Linton about Faithy's scratches," said Grandma Lolly.

"No! Don't tell Papa," I begged. Talk about trouble in the amen corner!

"But I should. Perhaps she needs special medicine."

"Noooooo," said Great Granny Blue Haired Lilac. "Come here child," she said, and I stood beside the wheelchair. Great Granny dabbed my wounds with red medicine she said was a home remedy, which burned like fire ants but soon dulled the bites. She rubbed a paste of turmeric into my hand and wrist wounds. It looked and smelled like mustard which I hate, but I bit my tongue.

Around the supper table Grandma Lolly fished for the truth one last time.

And it was one time too many. Because Little Lilly is too young to keep secrets, too young to lie and the rest of us are too worn out to play dodge ball.

"So where were y 'all when you got the lynx, Lilly?" She asked.

Everybody talked at once. Grandma Lolly held up a hand.

"I asked Lilly," said Grandma Lolly.

 And then Reader, truth and consequences kicked in.

For Little Lilly cried, "Faithy found him in a bawoil. When we are riding on the ribber in a canoe boat. Faithy fell in the ribber. Budgie, me Doobie and Faithy Jane, we about dwownded!" She finished with "Wahhhh, wahhh!"

"Faithy was brave," said Doobie, grabbing at straws. "Turns out she is brave."

"Ain't 'posed to go on the river," said Grandpa Liston. "I'll get my belt."

And, Reader, we got our due! Now you must know this was my first spanking!

Why, Mama and Papa have never even looked cross-eyed at me, much less spanked me! Mama will not hear of it, and I mind Papa to a "t". I am a perfectly (spoiled) good as gold child! Why, I won those Miss Citizenship pins! I am top reader! Now this!

I have always (I feel) acted mature, which is how children act when they have no siblings. I feel like I never was a little kid. I know I'm nine point five but when you are sick you grow up fast. I've never given anyone a reason to spank me. I've never done anything outrageous in my life!   At least I don't think so, till now!

But ho! Grandma Lolly can't pick out one for special treatment, now can she? I am in the gang, am I not? I am one of this club, this tribe, which calms me down a bit. In fact, I am not afraid, not terrified and not sweating. Well, maybe a little. But I am almost smiling when I realize I have lost a truckload of fear somewhere along this way.

I took my due "like a girl" because being part of the River Tribe Satilla is worth it and I mean really, what choice did I have? The idea of belonging, of my newly found freedom was and is an awesome feeling. Something happened deep inside me in a place I never knew existed. I had begun to feel foot loose and fancy free as the Oak Ridge Boys hit song goes (mama listened to it all the time, this is how I knew it) and I felt included for the first time in my life. Even if it meant a tail whoopin'! Even if it meant a "spanking" test!

The three licks, like the wild adventures since Sunday night was not the end of the world. And the punishment may very well have hurt Grandpa Liston more than it did us, because it was only three taps on the fanny. I knew it would not be too bad because I had endured a snake test, a bird test, a window jumping test and a near drowning. The tests were not harder, in fact, easier. Grandpa says the tests of life get easier to pass.

And now I did not faint though I did flinch. Indeed, I took my licks like a Searocker! I did not cry a tear. Pride would not let me, Faithy Jane Searocker, do so much as whimper.

Nobody else did either. No kidding. We were now a tribe. Bonded with secrets between us and to me life could not get any better. Nothing else surely, could happen any bigger or more magnificent...because I suddenly belonged, although I'd gotten their sort of a rough road.

And if I belonged to a brave group of cousins then I had a fighting chance at a lot of things. I admit that before Easter Vacation week I had seen myself the smartest girl on the block. I thought myself a rung higher on the social scale than my country cousins and called them secret names— (I know, shame on me) --such as redneck and hillbilly. I even sometimes called them wild and dingbats, yes, Miss Citizenship. I know name calling isn't good. But before, I couldn't help it. I had been a closet meanie, a snob sort of. No kidding.

My attitude needed an adjustment and it had just gotten one!

In two days, I had learned the difference between smart and wise, enemy and friend. It had been a lesson in friendship.

I had been through a series of tests, like football players go through if they make the team. I passed and made this team of country cousins! Woo.

But I had one more lesson to learn. One final lesson and it turned out to be the biggest lesson of them all, a lesson in blind trust. And Reader, it will come from a ...a... I CANNOT say it...Reader, please, JUST TURN THE PAGE!

Chapter 11

One Story Ends and Another Begins

After our whooping we young 'uns took a hot bath and eat supper. It is hard as heck to know how bone weary; we were unless you've been there, done that. We were flat out exhausted or as we say in 5th grade (where I'm going next year) ragged out.

Since Great Granny Blue Haired Lilac did not believe in medicine, for the first time in my life I got no pills. I got iodine and Sassafras tea and rubbed down, as all of us did, with the mustard paste and stuff I could not identify but which was homemade.

When the iodine was later poured onto my wounds Great Granny Blue Haired Lilac smiled and said, "No pain, no gain!" And I thought, Yeah, right, right and RIGHT! Ouch, ouch and Ouch!

Following our licks, we piled into beds and sleeping bags.

Budgie and Little Lolly slept with me.

"Faithy, are you asleep?" Budgie said, next to me in the feather bed.

"Yes. And Little Lilly's snoring," I whispered, "And kicking."

"She ought to be. She told on us!"

We laughed. Budgie is laughing *with* me, not *at* me.

"Doobie just rolled under the bed," Budgie says. "Don't say anything."

"I know. I heard him. Having a brother must drive you batty?" I said.

"Yeah, but he is a cool kid in the pack house," she says, "In school."

"I wish I had a brother. I've got a best friend, Uveda, but no one, well, you know how life is," I said, yawning.

Doobie kicked the bed. "Y 'all hush. I'm trying to sleep."

"No, you're not. You're warming up for something," says Budgie. "If you'll go to sleep you can stay. But any tricks and you're outta here."

In a little while the bedroom door opened and the thin shadows of Tee and Jee slid beneath the bed. But none of them said a word or made a noise all night long.

Which would have been fine, had someone NOT needed to awaken during the night. Naturally, nobody woke up but yours truly, as fate was not finished with me.

When the country night was heavy as a blanket with silence cut fourscore from now, I woke up and paddy padded to the kitchen for a drink of water. I opened the door and suddenly my feet were nailed to the oak floor! There at the table sat a lady eating a plate of leftovers fit for a queen. At first, I gasped, Golly, a ghost!

She looked down at her food and smiled. She wore a gold *Hermes* (No kidding) scarf around her gray hair tied in a knot beneath her pointed chin, a long sleeve shirt, a floral print skirt to her ankles and black boots with fur around the tops.

She looked up and our eyes caught. Hers sparkled like stars. She wore pearls around her neck which reminded me my pearls were in the river. So, what material things, I thought, mesmerized.

She jumped up and opened her arms. Chill bumps raced up and down my spine. I wanted to flee but could not. I was rooted to the spot.

"Faithy, you look wonderful!" she said, "Oh beauty, it's been a long a time."

Had I seen her before? Who is she and what does she want? How does she make me feel warm and welcome? Like meeting a friend, I have known since before the world was. Why was I not running for my life?

Like reading my mind she whispered, "Do you not remember me? My name is Loon." I thought she said Lee Ann but then realized, no, Loon!

Like a robot I walked into her arms for a hug. Her bright eyes illuminated the dimly lit kitchen. She looked like a movie star from an old two-tone film.

She said, "Honey, you hungry?"

I said, "Just water."

She handed me a drink of water. Then she took me by the

hand (hers were pale and felt paper thin) and led me outside.

We sat down in the wooden swing beneath an oak tree. She

seemed in a hurry and I thought it was because the others

might wake.

Grandpa Liston's rooster, Yellow Boy, slept in this tree but he did not notice.

The dogs slept beneath the porch. They did not notice.

And with a full moon shining like a plug nickel and fireflies blinking Loon told me a story about beginnings and endings.

"Once upon a time," Loon said, "There was a girl so afraid of her own shadow she was called *Afraid of Shadow*. The spirit of fear lived in her heart."

"Um, cool. And Miss Loon, how do you know these things?" I asked softly.

"Shhhh child, you only need to know what is called legend."

Crickets rubbed music from their wings in the Georgia forest as she told me things my heart needed knowing. Loon adjusted the knot beneath her chin several times. She seemed deep in thought and now and then stared at the stars with pure adoration.

"The Satilla River, like all earth's rivers, is a mercy river.

It goes to the sea. It is a loan not a gift. Hurt it not," she says, "The tall pines and oaks, my goodness they're wonderful gifts." Her face had a white glow.

I said softly, "I saw an eagle." She was right, I had seen a gift.

Loon smiled. "Eagles, trees, woods, all are gifts on loan. Hurt them not," she whispered again, motioning with the palm of her hand toward the forests. "Trees are why we have rain when we need it and why birds sing, and animals have homes."

I nod, watching Loon cross her legs and wondered about her boots since it wasn't winter. As though reading my mind, Loon says, "I am planted by the river, child. Near Harper Church so to get here, I must cross the creek on a foot log." She laughs. "And sometimes I fall in. I wear these to keep my feet from getting wet."

Loon claps her hands and says, "Now back to *Afraid of Shadow*."

"Now *Afraid of Shadow* wasn't friends with life, so life passed her by. You see, child, life will not live, where it isn't welcome. Friends will not darken your door if the door is never open." She smiled, patted my hand. I shiver as she talks about me.

"Ohhhhhhhh, I see," I whispered. And I saw.

"Fear is a deep canyon one falls into. Love is a bridge one walks across."

"Oh, I see," I said again, seeing yes, seeing.

"*Afraid of Shadow* lived a lonely life. She had no friends because she was too afraid to become a friend herself. She never went anywhere because she was afraid to travel. She never won anything because she was afraid to try."

"Oh," I said. I hung my head in shame of how afraid I had been of doing things I wanted to do out of fear I could not. Fear of failure! Fear of flunking life's tests!

Loon's eyes sparkled. And Reader, she says, "So one day while out on the river in a small canoe, a voice came to *Afraid of Shadow* and said, live, child, live, be brave for I give courage to you."

Loon places her hands on either side of my head and says,

"Child, you and I once played among the stars. Like all God's children, we knew each other before we came to live on this earth. I am the friend called spirit. You will always have me. You will always feel my courage. Live while you live."

I am crying now and jump up. I dash behind Grandma Lolly's azalea bushes. I hide for a few moments, whimpering, astonished. My eyes widen as I pull the bush aside and look toward the swing. I wanted to hug her, but I was so stunned by her words my lips trembled and I could not speak.

Where was she? Where was Loon?

Reader, the swing was empty!

It rocked gently in the glow of the moon-bright night. I ran back to the house, stumbled as I climbed the steps and through the back door which I closed softly. I tip-toed down the hallway and opened the door. I slid into the bed beside Budgie who hasn't moved a hair.

On the other side of Budgie, Little Lilly snored and kicked covers.

I fell into a heavy sleep and when I awakened the next

morning I wondered if my visitor had been a dream? Had I
been sleepwalking? Had I seen a ghost?

I thought I might never know the answer. I remembered
Little Lilly saying how a hobo had once come into the house,
eaten and then left. But I had not asked questions.

 And I wasn't starting now. I mean, I could never tell my
cousins about the visit from Loon. I was just getting into their
circle here and didn't want them to think of me as a liar or a
coward anymore. I could not tell about Loon although it was
going to be hard to keep this a secret.

The next few days passed in a daze.

"Your daydreaming, Faithy Jane," said Grandma Lolly
more than once. This was followed by a head shake, like, I'll
swannee, that girl?

"She's just scatter-brained," Budgie said and we laughed.
We played monopoly and watched Grandpa Liston's television
set. The television picture was clear or not depending on the
weather and angle of the rabbit ears.

Due to my scratches and leech bites, Grandma Lolly let us

stay inside for a few days. Plus, the fact she wanted my injuries cleared up by the time Mama and Papa arrived for Easter service at Harper Church.

I regretted spending the rest of Easter Week vacation inside the house, but I enjoyed helping Great Granny Blue Haired Lilac with the lynx. The game warden, Billy Bob Hardee, dropped by and got a hot scolding from Great Granny Blue Haired Lilac about how she could raise the lynx if she wanted too. She reminded him that in these parts, family is everything!

She told the game warden how she and his great grandmother were first cousins and she'd appreciate him not mentioning the lynx to the higher ups.

To which the game warden agreed since the lynx was too tiny to put back in the woods on its own. "But he's endangered, he's endangered," shouted Billy Bob Hardee over supper and left in a huff and said at the last he was satisfied Great Granny Blue Haired Lilac can raise the lynx real fine. Great Granny names the lynx Faithy.

On the night before Easter Sunday, Mama and Papa arrived late and go straight to bed, not knowing the stories of the past week, yet; too much going on. Thank you, Jesus, as my Grandpa Liston says.

Easter Sunday rolled up with Georgia sunshine brighter than a blueberry.

"Eggs!" shouted Little Lilly and we hunted eggs at sunrise in a wiregrass field near the ostrich pen. We hunted Easter eggs like hunting gold nuggets. We found half the eggs which some were cracked. We also found a rattle snake, a gopher tortoise and six Indian arrowheads plus one gold rock.

Following the egg hunt we rode to church in Grandpa Liston's pickup truck. The three grandparents crammed into the front and we young 'uns piled into the back, sitting on an old tire and dangling our feet from the tail gate. Little Lilly rode in Great Granny Blue Haired Lilac's wheelchair tied to the cab with an old rope.

"This is how we do it," Budgie said. She brushed her red bangs with the broken brush. "After church we'll walk home."

She smiled as though she had a secret which by now, you and I both, Reader, know she does.

I had been dying to tell Budgie about the visitor, but I had not. Because, since the near drowning my cousins treated me differently. They called me Sea ROCKER and Faithy Jane, queen of steel. They walked around me with respect and wonder of wonders, they shared everything. They had stopped picking on me, and I didn't call them names. Mainly, I had stopped fearing their country way of life. After all, they are family. They were and are my roots and reader, you can't dig up your roots like they never were. You can't change your history and you can't change the world's history!

During the church service I twisted in my seat, searching the faces. I wanted to see the woman who visited me. I wanted her to be real so I would know I hadn't been dreaming. I wanted, no, I knew all she had told me was true.

She was nowhere to be found.

After church, Budgie begged to walk home through a trail in the woods which leads from Harper Church across a narrow creek.

"Only if the boys walk with you," said Grandma Lolly.

Mama and Papa looked alarmed. Walk home? But they cave

in when Great Granny Blue Haired Lilac said, "We ain't

raising sissies. Sure, they can walk home."

And this is where the bridge walk began.

I called it a bridge walk because once I crossed this

"bridge" I answered one of the greatest mysteries of my life. I

found out who Loon was. And I found out who I am.

One story came to an end, and another began, like in a

great book.

Chapter 12

Goodbye Loon Hello Faithy

Harper Church is situated in a small valley at the end of a long dirt lane which runs beside the Satilla River. The road is what Georgia folks call "sand hill" and gophers and what all crawls everywhere. There are almost no flowers. Tall, long-leaf Yellow Pine trees shade the lane and magnificent live oak trees heavy with gray moss, shade the church yard. There is a sprinkling of azaleas and in the far back yard is a cactus plant nobody touches. The grown-ups tell the little kids to stay away from it because it will poke your eyes out.

Other than these stately trees and the white wooden clapboard Harper Church there is only one other thing: a graveyard sprawled like a gopher tortoise over the Georgia earth.

The graveyard covers an area the size of a corn field. Some of the tombstones are tall and ornate and date to the civil war. Some headstones are small. Some stones are long and wide with whole families laid to rest before them. Urns full of plastic flowers and what-nots line the graves. American flags fly.

Budgie picked a path through the tombstones and pointed out interesting graves.

"Here lies Bonnie Gail who Fell."

"Here lies Winston Who Talked the Horns Off a Billy Goat!"

"Seamus Has Gone --Leaving No One Behind"

"Troy Would Not Mind His Mama"

Little Lilly dashed from tombstone to tombstone, laying down wads of violets and seeds from pinecones. She sang at one tombstone, "Glory, Glory Hallelujah, his twooth marchin' on!" On a child's grave she placed a turtle shell.

We are almost out of the graveyard in an area which runs near a creek when reader, I see it: a tall ornate tombstone with a Celtic cross in the center. Something powerful draws me closer. It is like a magnet forcing me to come near.

My blood runs cold as I stop at the tombstone and read:

"Mattie Mae Loon Harper: Born 1788 - Died 1888 – She is an Angel Walking Among Us"

Doobie said, "She was our great Great- Great Granny. Way before our time. But Great Granny Blue Haired Lilac says she is still an angel who walks the river hills bringing messages from Heaven."

I swallow and nearly choke. I blink my eyes and feel tears.

Budgie said, "Great Granny Blue Haired Lilac swears Loon visits our house sometimes, in the night. She tells us stuff we need to know. She's the family ghost, ah, messenger. You know...an angel! Every families got one."

I felt pale and sat down, staring at the headstone. I rubbed my hand over the name.

"Why, have you seen her?" Budgie asked, shaking my arm. Doobie, Roper, Skeeterhawk, Tee and Jee and Little Lilly gathered around me, listening, staring from me to the tombstone and back to me again.

Budgie added, "Some have met her. I have not."

"Sea ROCKER! You've met Loon!" Doobie shouted.

"Cool."

And Reader, my country cousins pulled me up by both hands and we linked arms, leaving the gopher turtle back sprawling graveyard behind, walking down the red clay river road. Not a care in the world, blue Georgia skies and our minds reeling those scenes of the past week over and over like an old movie in school.

The air was thick with the scent of honeysuckle and wild Cherokee roses, and in the distance hound dogs yapped, yapped and yapped!

We walked about a mile through the woods, where I stopped crying and showed them what I had found lying on the grave by the headstone with Loon's name. Reader, please don't cry!

My lost pearls on a brand-new string.

And Reader, this is how I know that angels are real.

Review Request!

IF you LOVED this book, then I'd appreciate you giving it a great review (5 stars) on AMAZON...every review does help! Just go to this link...www.amazon.com/TheWildAdventuresOf Faithy. and click on customer review. Either one line or two or more would help but keep it brief and keep the writing clear...and I need to thank you, so THANKS IN ADVANCE!

Please visit my website at www.peggymercerworlwide.com and check out all the other fun stuff I've got going, about other books and all sorts of things. And please get in touch with me by letters or email, if you would like, and let me know if you like this story!

About the Author

Peggy Mercer is an award-winning author of Bestselling Books for children and young adults. She won Georgia Author of the Year, in 2011, for her early reader, ***Peach, When the Well Run Dry*** which is also sold in Washington, D.C., by the Children's Defense Fund...and she has written many other titles.

She loves writing for children and she bases her stories on real events...most of this crazy stuff really happened! She lives in the Georgia backwoods with a cat, Easter, and a bossy dog named Rocket and a variety of frogs, birds and foxes.

She also writes songs and owns a Music Publishing Company affiliated with BMI records. Her songs are recorded in Nashville, Tennessee and she helps other aspiring authors and songwriters develop their talents. She is also a ghostwriter for celebrities!

Send her an email or a note and she will respond:

peggyjunemercer@gmail.com

Made in the USA
Columbia, SC
04 June 2020